The Carters
Katie Night

The Carters
Copyright © 2024 by Katie Night

All rights reserved. No part of this book may be reproduced, stored in a retrieval system, or transmitted in any form or by any means—electronic, mechanical, photocopying, recording, or otherwise—without prior written permission from the publisher, except for brief quotations in reviews or articles.

ISBN- 979-8-3485-4488-1

Cover design by Author's Aura
Interior design by Katie Night

This is a work of fiction. Any resemblance to actual persons, living or dead, events, or locations is purely coincidental.

First Edition: August, 2024

This book contains scenes that may depict, mention, or discuss: Depression on paper, Infertility on paper & historical, BDSM on paper (Female Dominant, Male Submissive), Whipping on paper (sexual punishment), Pegging, Therapy.

Contents

Dedication		VII
1.	Erica	1
2.	Brian	7
3.	Erica	14
4.	Brian	22
5.	Brian	30
6.	Erica	36
7.	Brian	45
8.	Erica	51
9.	Brian	60
10.	Erica	66
11.	Brian	71
12.	Erica	79
13.	Brian	84
14.	Erica	91
15.	Brain	95
16.	Erica	103
17.	Brian	108

18.	Erica	117
19.	Brian	122
20.	Erica	128
21.	Brian	134
22.	Erica	139
23.	Brian	143
24.	Brian	149
25.	Erica	154
26.	Erica	159
27.	Brian	163
28.	Erica	168
29.	Brian	171
30.	Erica	177
31.	Erica	183
32.	Brian	189
33.	Brain	196
34.	Erica	199
35.	Brian	204
Epilogue		210
Acknowledgements		221
About the author		223

For my beautiful, strong, and selfless best friend.
Know that I see you, I see the pain you try to hide to be in my life. I love you.

To anyone who is, or has suffered from infertility, you are not alone.

Your happy ending may not be what you pictured, but it's still that; a happy ending.

Chapter 1

Erica

I can't do this anymore.

The pressure is suffocating, wrapping around me like a vice. My hands shake as I zip my last bag, my vision blurred by the tears streaking down my face. I take a deep breath, forcing myself to double-check that I have everything before hauling the suitcase to my car.

One more thing. The note.

I've spent days agonizing over what to write, rewriting the same painful words over and over. But there's no perfect way to say, *I love you, but I have to leave.*

I glance around the house—our house—one last time before grabbing the first of my bags and heading outside. My black Ford Expedition sits in the driveway, its presence grounding me just enough to take the next step. My mind drifts as I turn back for the rest of my things.

Five years of marriage. One year of trying. And nothing to show for it but heartbreak.

When Brian and I first decided to start a family, we were full of hope. We whispered about baby names at night, dreamed about nurseries, imagined tiny feet padding across these floors. But somewhere along the way, that hope turned into pressure.

Sex became a job, a task dictated by ovulation trackers and fertility windows. Spontaneity disappeared. Passion faded. The only time we touched was when the calendar told us to, and even then, I felt nothing but emptiness.

And every month, when another test came back negative, that emptiness grew.

The world around me seemed to mock my pain—friends and coworkers announcing pregnancies with effortless joy, family members offering well-meaning but unbearable advice. And then came the pity. The sympathetic glances. The quiet whispers.

"When will you two start trying?"

"Have you thought about seeing a specialist?"

"It'll happen when the time is right."

I smile. I nod. I pretend it doesn't hurt.

But it does. It hurts so damn much.

I know Brian doesn't mean to make it worse. He's just excited, hopeful in a way I can't bring myself to be anymore. In the beginning, he was always the first to suggest taking a test, asking eagerly if I'd checked yet—until I snapped, telling him I didn't need a reminder of my own failure.

He never asked again.

Then one night, he suggested we take a step back. That maybe we should stop trying for a while. He said it was because of the stress, because he hated seeing what this was doing to me. And maybe that was true.

But all I heard was, *You're not enough.*

That was the moment something shifted between us. I withdrew. He pulled away. Conversations turned into small talk. Laughter faded into silence. Most nights, he slept in the spare bedroom.

I know it's not fair. I know this isn't his fault. But I also know that if I stay, I'll start to resent him. Maybe I already have.

We never talk about what happens if we *can't* have a baby. The possibility hangs between us, unspoken and unbearable. We both know the conversation needs to happen, but neither of us can bring ourselves to say the words.

And if I don't even know how to answer that question, how can I expect Brian to?

The last bag is packed. The car is full. All that's left is the note.

The house is quiet, but my mind is loud.

I sit at the dining room table, fingertips tracing the smooth wooden surface, my chest tight with indecision. The half-packed suitcases in my car feel like an anchor, pulling me in two different directions.

I pick up the pen, press it to the notepad, and start to write. Then stop.

Tearing off the ruined page, I toss it onto the growing pile of crumpled attempts. I try again. And again. But no words feel right. How do I explain something I barely understand myself?

I lean back in my chair, exhaling shakily, and let my thoughts wander—back to before everything became so complicated. Back to when Brian and I weren't just trying to conceive but were simply *in love*.

Back when we couldn't keep our hands off each other.

No tracking periods, no temperature readings, no fertility apps dictating when we *should* be intimate. Just the raw, desperate pull between two people who wanted each other completely.

I close my eyes, and suddenly, I'm there again—at my sister's house, celebrating my parents' thirtieth wedding anniversary.

I had slipped away from the party unnoticed, my pulse thrumming with excitement as I texted Brian:

> **Come upstairs. I need you.**

When he finally found me in the upstairs bathroom, I barely gave him time to shut the door before I was on him. Our lips collided, my hands fisting the front of his shirt as I pulled him closer.

He groaned against my mouth, backing me up against the sink. His strong hands lifted me effortlessly, placing me on the cool marble counter. My dress made it easy—no zippers, no buttons—just his fingers slipping beneath the hem, pushing my panties aside, and sliding into me in one smooth stroke.

A gasp tore from my throat, my legs wrapping around him as he filled me, his body pressing me firmly against the counter.

"Look at yourself," he murmured, voice thick with lust. "I want you to see how perfect you look falling apart around my cock."

His words sent a shiver down my spine. He pulled me off the counter and turned me around, bending me over the sink. The mirror reflected my flushed cheeks, my parted lips, the hunger in his eyes as he thrust into me from behind.

I remember the way he gripped my hips, how each deep stroke sent waves of pleasure crashing through me. How I had to bite my lip to keep from crying out, knowing our family was just downstairs.

It didn't take long before I shattered around him, my body trembling as I came. Brian followed moments later, burying himself deep as he groaned my name into my skin.

I inhale sharply, my eyes snapping open, the memory fading like smoke.

God, we used to be *so good* together.

Now, everything is about getting pregnant. It's not just the pressure I feel from Brian—it's the pressure I put on myself. The way I measure my worth by the single pink line on a pregnancy test.

We agreed to try naturally for as long as we could handle it. But I don't know if conceiving would even fix us anymore.

We don't talk. And when we do, it's about logistics—work schedules, grocery lists, arguments waiting to happen. Most nights, he sleeps in the spare bedroom. Unless I'm ovulating. Then he comes to bed with me. But even those nights are happening less and less.

We talked about seeing a fertility specialist—maybe by the end of the year. But before I can even consider that, I need to figure out if I can do this anymore. If I can keep holding onto something that feels like it's already slipping through my fingers.

I don't blame Brian. This isn't his fault. It's not mine, either.

But I still feel like I'm failing.

My phone buzzes in my back pocket. I pull it out and see a text from my mom:

Let me know when you're on your way.

I hesitate for only a moment before typing back:

Leaving now.

I'll be staying with my parents for the summer. They live two hours away, and since I'm a web designer, and my job is remote, I have the time. Time to breathe. Time to think.

I glance at the notepad again and pick up the pen.

Brian,

I am so sorry. I couldn't bring myself to tell you this in person because I knew you'd talk me out of it.

I need time. Time to clear my head. Time to figure out if this is still what I want.

I'm going to stay with my parents for a while. Please don't come after me. When I'm ready, I'll reach out.

—Erica

Tears well in my eyes, but I blink them back, hoping they won't fall onto the page. It's too late. A few stray drops smudge the ink.

It doesn't matter. The message is still clear.

I push back from the table, grab my keys, and toss the failed notes into the trash. With one final glance around the house—the home we built together—I step out the door.

The second I slide into the driver's seat, my breath catches in my throat.

This is real.

I grip the wheel, squeeze my eyes shut, and force myself to take a steadying breath.

And then, before I can second-guess myself, I put the car in reverse, back out of the driveway, and leave.

I don't know what's waiting for me on the other side of this.

But I know I can't stay.

Chapter 2

BRIAN

The weight settles in my chest before I even leave the office.

I loosen my tie, roll my shoulders, but the tension won't ease. It never does. Not anymore. I know exactly why.

By now, Erica is probably home. It's close to the time she ovulates, which means tonight is one of *those* nights—the ones marked on the calendar, planned down to the minute. The ones that feel more like an obligation than an act of love.

Sex used to be easy with Erica. It used to be fun. Passionate. Messy. We'd steal moments between meetings, barely make it through dinner before we were pulling each other upstairs, tangled in sheets, breathless with laughter.

Now? Now it's scheduled. Clinical.

I still want my wife. Of course I do. But somewhere between tracking cycles and counting fertile days, the spark faded. Every touch, every kiss—it's all measured against a single goal: conception. And if it doesn't happen, the disappointment lingers in the air like a storm cloud.

I grip the steering wheel tighter as I drive home.

I know Erica feels the pressure. I do, too. But I never wanted *this*—for our entire relationship to be consumed by trying. I told her once that maybe we should take a step back, stop forcing it. She took it as me giving up.

That fight was the worst we'd ever had.

That was the night I started sleeping in the spare bedroom.

It wasn't meant to be permanent, but the space between us only grew. Conversations became strained, short, empty. The only time we touched was when her fertility app told us it was time. Even then, some nights, she didn't reach for me at all.

I saw how much it was weighing on her, but I failed to see just how deep it went. I didn't understand—not at first. Not until two of her coworkers announced their pregnancies in the same week.

Not until our family started asking, "*When will it be your turn?*"

They didn't know. They had no idea that we had already been trying. That every negative test was another fracture in Erica's heart.

She threw herself into research—fertility diets, supplements, vitamins. I went along with it, because what else could I do? We changed everything, hoping something would work.

Nothing did.

And then, just when I thought it couldn't get worse, her sister got pregnant.

That was the breaking point. The endless questions from family, the unsolicited advice, the sympathetic looks.

Since then, things have never been the same.

We talked about seeing a specialist, but I kept dragging my feet. Not because I didn't want to try—because I was scared.

What if it's me?

What if I'm the reason we can't have a baby?

Worse—what if they tell Erica she'll never get pregnant? I *hope* it's me, because I can't bear the thought of her carrying that pain alone.

I exhale sharply and turn into the driveway.

Erica's car isn't here.

That's unusual, but maybe she had a meeting that ran late. She's been overwhelmed with work lately. Maybe that's all it is.

I head inside, toeing off my shoes before walking upstairs. I could use a shower—maybe then I'll feel less like I'm suffocating.

As the water heats, I reach for my phone and order dinner. If Erica is home by the time it arrives, we can sit down and eat together. Maybe tonight can be normal.

Steam billows from the shower as I step in, letting the hot water loosen my muscles. I grab my bar of soap, the woodsy scent filling the air, grounding me.

For a few minutes, I let myself imagine a different version of us. One where Erica isn't drowning in grief. One where we don't tiptoe around each other, afraid to say the wrong thing.

One where she still looks at me the way she used to.

I scrub a hand down my face and shut off the water. The house is still eerily silent as I towel off, pull on a pair of shorts, and throw on a lightweight shirt. As I run a hand through my damp hair, I hear the doorbell ring.

Good. At least dinner is here. Maybe this night isn't completely ruined.

I head downstairs, grab the food, and carry it to the kitchen. I plate everything, making sure to get Erica's drink just how she likes it—sparkling water in a glass with ice.

It's a small thing, but it's something.

I move everything to the dining room, setting it up the way we used to before our world became centered around ovulation tests and scheduled sex.

I glance at the clock.

She should be home by now.

Where the hell is she?

I glance back at the food, perfectly in place on the table. That's when I see it.

A single sheet of paper.

My name is written across the top in Erica's handwriting.

A strange sense of unease creeps up my spine as I reach for it. My hands are steady, but my heart is not.

I scan the words, barely breathing.

Brian,

I am so sorry. I couldn't bring myself to tell you this in person...

The rest of the letter blurs as the meaning sinks in.

She's gone.

She's *gone*.

She's not at work. She's not running errands. She's not coming home.

I grip the edge of the table, trying to steady the sudden rush of nausea twisting in my gut. How did I not see this coming? Have things really been so bad that I became numb to her silence? To her absence?

I drop into the chair, my legs suddenly weak beneath me. My phone is in my hand before I even register grabbing it.

Her name is right there on the screen.

Do I call? Do I fight for her? Or do I respect the space she's asking for and hope to God she comes back to me?

My finger hovers over her name, but I hesitate. I don't know what to say. I don't know what I'm supposed to do. Before I can decide, my phone vibrates.

For one fleeting second, hope surges through me. Maybe it's Erica. Maybe she's changed her mind. Maybe she's coming home.

But then my mother's name flashes across the screen.

I consider ignoring it, but my body moves on autopilot. I bring the phone to my ear.

"Hello, Mom."

"Hello, dear! Are you and Erica still planning on coming next weekend?" she asks, her voice light, casual—completely oblivious to the fact that my world is shattering around me. "Your sister will be there with the kids."

I swallow hard. I have to tell her.

"Ma," I try, but she barrels on.

"Oh! And your brother's bringing his new girlfriend. Your aunt—"

"Mom." My voice is sharp, cutting through her excitement. "Erica won't be there. I don't think she'll be coming to anything for a while."

The words taste bitter on my tongue. My marriage is falling apart, and this is how I have to say it out loud for the first time.

There's a pause. Then a sigh. "Oh, don't tell me it's because Stacy will be there. Brian, just because you two haven't gotten pregnant yet doesn't mean you can't come to family gatherings."

And just like that, I finally understand what Erica has been saying all along.

My mother doesn't *get it*.

She never has.

"Mom," I say, exhaling sharply, "if Erica doesn't want to go and be bombarded with questions about when we're having a baby, she doesn't have to. Besides, she won't even be here."

Silence.

"What do you mean?" she finally asks, her voice no longer light. "I just spoke to her last week, and she said you'd both be coming."

My throat tightens. "Yeah, well... she left." The confession feels like a punch to the ribs. "She's staying with her parents for a while. We're... taking some time apart."

My mother sucks in a breath. "Time apart?" There's no more dismissal in her voice—just concern now. "What does that mean, Brian?"

"It means..." I drag a hand down my face. "It means I need to figure out how to fix this. It means I don't know if I *can* fix this."

A heavy silence stretches between us.

"Brian," she says gently.

"I don't want to talk about it," I cut in. "Not right now."

She hesitates. "Okay," she finally concedes. "I just—I love you. You know that, right?"

My chest tightens.

"Yeah," I murmur. "I love you too."

Before she can say anything else, I end the call.

The weight of it all finally crushes me.

I grip my phone tighter—then hurl it across the room with a sharp, angry shout.

How could I have been so *blind*?

How did I not see how much pressure Erica was under? How did I not realize we had been drifting apart so badly that she felt like she had no choice but to leave?

I sink forward, elbows braced on my knees, my head in my hands.

She's gone.

And I don't know if she's ever coming back.

Chapter 3

Erica

It's been one week since I left Brian.

Seven days.

One hundred and sixty-eight hours.

And I miss him.

For the most part, he's respected my need for space. He hasn't bombarded me with calls or begged me to come home. Instead, his texts have been few, simple, restrained.

Like the one that just came in.

I miss you.

That's it. Nothing more. No please. No questions. Just three words that squeeze around my heart like a fist.

I stare at the message for too long before locking my phone and setting it aside. If I keep looking, I'll end up texting him back. And I can't. Not yet.

I glance around my childhood bedroom—the one my mom turned into her office but never really changed. The purple-and-blue comforter still covers my full-sized bed, the same posters still hang on the walls, and one of my favorite stuffed animals—a sloth my grandpa gave me before he passed—rests beside my pillow.

I've clung to it a lot since coming back. Like now.

Hugging it to my chest, I scroll through Brian's other messages.

The first few were desperate, begging me to talk to him. Then they turned softer—photos of little things that reminded him of me. A sunrise from our bedroom window. A coffee cup from my favorite shop. A book I left on my nightstand.

Each dawn, he texts good morning.

Every dusk, he texts goodnight.

I squeeze my eyes shut, my throat tightening. I need to put my phone away before I give in.

With a frustrated groan, I throw myself back onto the bed, covering my face with my sloth. Then, because no one is around to hear, I let out a muffled scream.

God, this *hurts*.

I thought leaving would make things clearer. That I'd feel some sense of relief. But all I feel is this aching, hollow space where Brian used to be.

He's always been my person—the one who made everything easier, more manageable. But these last few months, being around him only made the weight on my chest heavier. Like he was looking at me differently.

Like I was letting him down.

I know I should have talked to him before it got this bad. But I was scared. What if he really does see me differently? What if I've already lost him?

I shake the thought away and force myself upright. I can't keep lying here, wallowing. I need to get out of this house. I push off the bed and head down the hall to the guest bathroom, flipping on the light. The dark walls with bright white accents still surprise me. It's a stark contrast to the soft sage and cream it used to be.

Some things change.

Some things stay the same.

I move to the linen closet, rummaging through shelves for candles, bath salts, bubble bath—anything to help me breathe. My fingers brush over a folded towel, and I smirk. A towel warmer? Mom must have upgraded.

At least one thing is going right today.

Armed with everything I need, I step back into the bathroom and start running the tub. I add a handful of citrus-scented bath salts, watching as they dissolve into the steaming water, then pour in the matching bubble bath.

While the tub fills, I go through my routine—pinning my hair up, dry-brushing my skin, applying an under-eye mask. Anything to make myself feel a little more put together.

When the bath is high enough, I slip out of my nightgown, tossing it down the laundry chute, and ease into the water.

The second the heat surrounds me, I realize just how tense I've been.

I sink deeper, letting the warmth work its way into my stiff muscles, letting the scent of citrus clear my head.

For the first time in a week, I breathe.

A real, deep, cleansing breath.

And for the first time in months, I feel a sliver of calm.

I tip my head back, eyes fluttering shut, and let my thoughts drift.

At first, I make a mental checklist—things to do today, things to keep me busy. The weekend farmers market with my mom and sister. Fresh produce for dinner. Strawberries and honey at the top of my list.

Then, work. I need to check in with my team, schedule the upcoming virtual meeting, and rearrange my planner to make working from my parents' house easier.

The more I plan, the lighter I feel.

Then, inevitably, my mind circles back to Brian.

To us.

I don't know what to do. I don't want my marriage to end, but I also don't know how we can keep going like this. I know Brian loves me. I know that. But how could he still want to be with me if I can't give him the one thing he's wanted his whole life?

With that last thought, another one slips in—one I haven't allowed myself to linger on in a long time.

One of our first dates.

It must have been our second or third. I had insisted on asking more questions, wanting to get to know him better. So we made a game of it—each of us coming up with five questions for the other.

One of mine was: *Where do you see yourself in five years?*

Brian answered immediately. He saw himself as a marketing researcher for the publishing company he worked for—he holds that title now. The thought makes me smile. He's always been so driven, so determined to carve out the life he wanted.

I scoop up a handful of bubbles, blowing them into the air, watching them dance before they disappear. But my mind drifts back to that night.

He didn't just talk about his career. He said he saw himself married. Either already with children, or at the very least, expecting one.

"I've always wanted to be a father," he had admitted, his voice full of quiet certainty.

He spoke about his own dad, how much joy parenthood had brought him, how he always said there was no greater feeling than watching your child grow and succeed.

At the time, I had smiled, thinking it was just one more thing we had in common. But now, looking back, I realize something I missed then.

He hadn't just been sharing his dreams.

He had been telling me something.

He wasn't just saying he wanted kids—he was telling me he was *ready*. That at twenty-six, he wasn't just dating for fun. He was looking for a future, for this future.

For me.

I exhale, sinking deeper into the water.

That was also the night we first touched each other intimately. I remember the way he kissed his way down my neck, both of us still fully dressed. I remember the way his hands trembled as he tried to unbutton my shirt.

"I've never done this before," he confessed softly, his breath warm against my skin.

I had rolled my eyes, thinking it was just a line—until I saw the hesitation in his eyes. The nervous energy humming through his fingertips.

He was serious.

I stopped him then, my hands covering his, assuring him we didn't have to do anything he wasn't comfortable with.

But he had only kissed me deeper, his lips lingering against my throat as he whispered, "I just want to taste you."

A shiver rolls through me despite the warmth of the bath.

I can still see the way his brows pulled together in confusion when I lightly pushed him back. He had opened his mouth to speak, but I silenced him with a single touch of my finger against his lips.

I wanted him to watch me.

I sat up on my knees, slowly undoing the buttons of my blouse, one by one, never breaking eye contact.

He didn't move. Didn't even breathe.

His gaze followed my hands as I shrugged the fabric from my shoulders, then reached for the clasp of my skirt. The way his throat bobbed, the way his green eyes darkened with hunger—it made my own pulse stutter.

He was pinned in place by the moment. And so was I.

Then, as if breaking free from a spell, he rose to his knees, pulling me into him. My nipples tightened as the warmth of his body pressed against mine. As if he could sense my need, he cupped my breast in his palm, groaning at the feel of me. And his mouth crashed against mine, lips and tongues dancing in a searing kiss.

I inhale sharply, my own hand rising from the bathwater to tease my breast, mirroring that moment.

I recall the way he had stopped me when I tried to reach for him, whispering, "Tonight is about you."

The way he laid me back, hands and mouth exploring, gaining confidence with every sound I made. The way he had finally, *finally* slid his fingers under my skirt, his fingertips tracing over the lace of my panties. Instinctively, I arched my back into him, inviting him to take my nipple into his mouth as his hands pushed my skirt up.

He took me in, and I took the opportunity to run my eyes over his figure, catching on his sizable erection, evidence of his want for me.

"You are truly beautiful," he said huskily, his darkening gaze drinking me in. His palms ghosted up my legs again—this time all the way to the hem of my panties. His hesitation only made the butterflies in my stomach flutter more. I saw the moment he decided to continue; his jaw ticked, and then he pulled them down, exposing me to him.

A nervous energy coiled inside me. This was the furthest he'd ever gone with anyone. And though he wasn't my first, he was the first to make me feel like this.

I had never been able to climax with a partner. They never put me first.

But he had.

"You'll have to tell me what to do—tell me what you like." His voice had been more of a plea than anything else.

So I did. I told him how I touched myself.

"Can I taste you? Will you tell me what to do?" he all but whispered.

All I managed was a nod before my breath hitched into a scream as he replaced his thumb with his mouth. The sound made him stop.

"Don't stop!" I gasped.

I felt him smile against my clit before resuming—swirling his tongue, lightly sucking.

"Use your finger like before," I instructed.

He obeyed instantly, sliding one inside me, curling it just right, listening to every sound I made, learning my body with eager reverence.

"Another," I had moaned.

He gave me what I needed without hesitation, taking my directions flawlessly.

"Yes—fuck, I'm going to—"

I had shattered around him, my body trembling, my mind lost to sensation.

And when I finally came down, when my body had stopped shaking, he had only pulled me into his arms, not asking for anything in return.

He just *held* me.

I drag my lip between my teeth, my body still humming from the memory.

Brian had always been that way—selfless, devoted, desperate to make me happy. But somewhere along the way, we stopped putting each other first. Somewhere along the way, we started drowning.

I let out a shaky breath, sinking deeper into the cooling water.

I don't want my marriage to end. I don't want to lose him.

But I also don't know how to fix this.

All I know is that if I can't give him a child, things will never be the same. How could they be? How could he still want me if I can't give him the one thing he's always dreamed of?

The bath has gone cold, my skin chilled. With a sigh, I pull the drain, then turn on the shower to rinse away the lingering bubbles. I always do this—I've never felt truly clean after a bath. It's a habit I've had since I was young.

Now that I'm clean and my body is relaxed, I turn off the water and reach for the towel from the warmer, wrapping it tightly around myself. Only then do I realize I forgot to bring my clothes and robe with me. With a groan, I fasten the towel securely and pad back to my room.

Chapter 4

BRIAN

I barely recognize the man staring back at me. Dark circles shadow my eyes, my beard is overgrown, and the misery in my reflection is impossible to ignore.

It's only been a week since Erica left, and I'm barely holding on. I'm not sleeping. I'm barely eating. I can't focus on anything except the deafening silence of our house without her in it.

At first, I took a few personal days, thinking time alone would help. It didn't. Sitting in our home without her was worse than fighting with her. At least when we were fighting, *she was still here*.

I grip the sink, exhaling slowly.

I have to go to that stupid family gathering today. I'm not ready for the questions, the sympathetic looks, the not-so-subtle hints about when Erica and I will finally have a baby.

They don't know.

They don't know she's gone.

And I don't know how to tell them.

But if I don't go, my mother will never let me hear the end of it.

Pull yourself together.

I reach for my clippers, adjusting the guard before running them over my beard. Watching it fall into the sink feels symbolic—like shedding the week of grief I've been drowning in.

Once I'm done, I rinse the basin, turn on the shower, and lean against the counter while I wait for the water to heat.

How had I not seen this coming? How did I miss how unhappy she was?

My phone dings. My heart jumps before my brain catches up.

It won't be her.

It hasn't been her all week.

I glance down. *Mom*. Of course.

I don't even bother reading the message. Instead, I walk into our adjoining bedroom and toss the phone onto the bed.

The empty bed.

The bed that hasn't been slept in since she left.

Swallowing hard, I turn to my dresser, grabbing socks and boxers. Then I strip down, tossing my clothes into the hamper. Another reminder of how much my life has unraveled—I need to do laundry.

I head back into the bathroom, grabbing a towel from the cabinet before stepping into the shower. The second the hot water hits my skin, I tip my head back, letting it wash away some of the tension clinging to my muscles.

But it doesn't wash away *her*.

She's everywhere.

In my thoughts. In the spaces she used to fill. And no matter how hard I try, I can't stop thinking about her. One memory in particular sneaks in, one I haven't let myself think about in a long time.

The night I realized I was in love with her. The first night we made love.

I squeeze shampoo into my palm and scrub it into my hair, trying to focus on something—anything—else.

But I can still see her.

The way she looked at me that night. The way she felt under my hands.

I force myself to shake the memory away, rinsing the soap from my hair, reaching for my bar of soap, lathering it between my hands. Focusing on the simple, mechanical motions of washing up.

It mostly works.

Until I step out of the shower and into the closet.

Her scent hits me immediately. It lingers in the fabric of her clothes, in the air, wrapping around me like a ghost. She always used those scented laundry boosters she loved so much. But since my skin is sensitive, we did our laundry separately. I used to love the way her clothes smelled.

Now, it just reminds me that she's not here.

I inhale sharply, grabbing the first things I see—a pair of tan pants, a navy polo—and retreat back to the bedroom. Dressing quickly, I move back into the bathroom, squirting a small amount of gel into my hands and working it through my dark brown hair.

I style it like I always do—slightly messy, but still put together.

When I glance at my reflection, I look... better. But not right. Nothing about this feels right.

The dark circles under my eyes tell the truth—no matter how much I try to clean myself up, I'm still falling apart inside.

With a sigh, I grab my socks and head downstairs.

The sooner I get this damn family thing over with, the better.

The second I park outside my mom's house, regret settles deep in my gut.

I shouldn't have come.

I almost consider turning around, but I know that would only make things worse. My mother would call, then text, then show up at my door if I ignored this family gathering altogether.

Taking a deep breath, I pull the keys from the ignition but don't move. Instead, I grip the steering wheel and rest my forehead against it.

What is she doing right now?

Does she miss me?

What could I have done to make her stay?

My mind spirals, running through every scenario, every mistake, every moment I could have changed. I'm so lost in thought that I don't realize I've been lightly knocking my forehead against the wheel until a dull ache settles between my brows.

Frustrated, I exhale sharply, rolling my shoulders in an attempt to shake off the tension. It doesn't work. But I can't sit here all day. I step out of the car, hoping I can linger outside a little longer before facing everyone.

A honk makes me jump.

I look up just in time to see a neighbor drive by, waving. I lift a hand in return, but my movement stalls when I notice my mother standing in the doorway, arms crossed, eyes narrowed. I'm only thirty minutes late, but she looks at me like I've committed a crime.

Rolling my eyes, I trudge up the steps.

"Hi, Mom. Sorry I'm late. I overslept." I kiss her cheek as I step inside.

"I see Erica couldn't be bothered to show up."

Her voice is sharp, dismissive, and just like that, every ounce of patience I had evaporates. I clench my jaw, forcing myself to stay calm. She doesn't know. She doesn't understand.

"Mom, please don't start," I say, running a hand through my hair. "We already talked about why she couldn't make it. Please, just... let it be."

Something in my voice must strike a chord because she actually stops to look at me. Really look at me.

Her expression softens.

She exhales, reaching out to pull me into a hug. It's quick but comforting, and when she pulls away, she pats my cheek.

"I know, dear. I remember how I felt when your father ran off with his 'other' family." She sighs before gesturing toward the backyard. "Why don't you head outside? Your brother is manning the grill, and you know someone needs to supervise once he starts drinking his beers."

She turns back toward the kitchen, where she's immediately swept up in gossip and food prep.

I step onto the patio, scanning the yard until my eyes land on Stacy, my brother's wife. She's sitting in one of the lounge chairs, looking vaguely uncomfortable.

Her polite smile falters slightly when she sees me. Does she know?

"Hey, Stace. How are you?" I ask, leaning down to hug her.

"Oh, you know, just living the dream of pregnancy," she laughs, shifting in her seat. "Tired, sore, hot, and ready for this to be over."

She doesn't look tired—she looks radiant. Her honey-brown hair is twisted up into a messy bun, her yellow sundress light and flowing. Her bare feet are propped up on another chair, swollen ankles on full display.

"You don't have much longer, right?"

"Nine weeks. Hopefully less." She adjusts in her seat again before glancing toward the house. "Is Erica inside? I was hoping she made more of that jello and fruit thing she did last time—it sounds so good right now."

There it is. The question I've been dreading.

I run a hand through my hair, scrambling for an exit from this conversation, but there's none in sight.

"No, unfortunately, she couldn't make it today. Something came up." I switch subjects before she can push further. "Have you guys picked out names yet? I know John said you decided to wait to find out the gender."

It works.

For a second.

"No, we can't seem to agree on anything," she admits before grinning. "Which I'm sure you'll understand when you and Erica start a family."

And just like that, my stomach drops.

"Speaking of," she continues, eyes lighting up, "have you two talked about when you might start trying? It would be so fun for our little peanut to grow up with a cousin close in age."

I swallow hard.

"Oh, um, actually—"

A groan cuts me off.

"Oh, rats, not again!" She lifts her arms for help, and I oblige, helping her to her feet. "Excuse me, I have to pee for the millionth time today."

She waddles inside, leaving her shoes abandoned on the patio.

I sink into the seat she just vacated, rubbing my forehead.

That was one person asking about when we'd have a baby. One. And it still cracked something inside me. How does Erica deal with this all the time? How does she listen to people casually ask about something we want so badly but can't seem to have?

Her heart must be shattered.

I need a drink.

I push to my feet, heading inside, only to freeze when I hear my mother's voice carrying through the kitchen.

"I just don't understand her. She can't even be happy for John and Stacy?"

My stomach twists.

"Brian said she's staying at her parents' house."

I take another slow step forward, keeping myself out of sight.

"That's what I told him! It's ridiculous. She'll get pregnant soon. It's not like they've been trying that long."

I stop listening.

I stop feeling.

She doesn't know. None of them know.

We hadn't told anyone we were trying. We didn't want to take anything away from her sister's pregnancy. And then... nothing happened. So we stayed silent.

And now? Now, my mother is mocking her pain without even realizing it. I can't do this. I need to get out of here.

I stalk through the kitchen, heading for the front door, but my mother calls out before I can escape.

"Brian, there you are! Come help me take these out to the table."

I shake my head. No.

"Brian, where are you going?"

"Home, Mother."

She grabs my wrist before I can leave, pulling me into the study.

"What has gotten into you? You just got here!"

I spin to face her, my green eyes locking onto hers, anger simmering just beneath the surface.

"Yes, I did. And now I'm leaving."

"Brian, it's bad enough that Erica didn't come with you—"

I recoil like she's struck me.

"No, Mom. You listen to me." She blinks, startled by the sharpness in my voice. "Erica didn't come today, not because she isn't happy for John and Stacy, but because we've been trying for almost a *year*."

Her breath catches.

"She's tired of being asked when we'll have a baby. She's not ungrateful. She's not selfish. She's *hurting*." The words feel like knives in my throat. "And I was too stupid to see that. And now she's gone."

Silence.

"So no, I'm not staying today. Tell everyone I'm sorry. But I have to go."

This time, when I push past her, she lets me.

Once I'm outside, safe within the confines of my car, I pull out my phone and dial her number. Two rings.

Voicemail.

"Erica, baby. Please call me back. I love you."

I don't know what else to say. So I hang up and drive back to my cold, empty house.

Chapter 5

BRIAN

It's been four months.

Four months since Erica left. One hundred and twenty-one days of waking up alone.

I still text her every morning and every night. *Good morning. Good night. I miss you.* She replies sometimes, but lately, her messages feel... distant. Forced. Like she's just being polite.

Like she's already slipping away.

I try to stay hopeful, but it's getting harder with each passing day.

I send my usual morning text, then toss my phone onto the bed.

I don't sleep in our bedroom anymore. At first, it was because I physically couldn't—I would just lie there, staring at the ceiling, waiting for her to come back. So I moved to the guest room, thinking it might help.

It doesn't.

Sleeping in there makes me feel like an outsider in my own home. But at least it's better than waking up in the bed we picked out together. The bed where we made love a thousand times.

I groan, draping an arm over my face to block out the morning light.

I try not to think about her. About us. About what it felt like to have her curled up beside me at night. But my body betrays me.

It happens every morning—waking up painfully hard, my body reacting to the absence of hers.

I squeeze my eyes shut, willing the ache to pass. It doesn't.

I've tried taking care of it. But lately, it only pisses me off. No matter how many times I jerk off, nothing helps. Nothing scratches the itch. It used to be a way to take the edge off in between ovulations, something to tide me over until we could try again.

Now? Now, it just reminds me of what I don't have.

Of *who* I don't have.

Frustrated, I rake a hand through my brown hair, tugging slightly at the roots. The sharp pinch of pain is supposed to ground me, pull me from my dark thoughts. Instead, it just makes me harder.

Fuck this.

I shove the blankets aside and head straight to our bedroom, an idea forming in my mind as I go. The second I step inside, I make a beeline for Erica's dresser. I pull open the drawer and grab one of her nightgowns—her favorite one. The light pink one with white polka dots, trimmed in black lace, with tiny bows decorating the straps.

She looked so damn good in it.

It was just long enough to be teasing but short enough to make me crazy. She used to wear it on purpose, flaunting around the house, pretending she didn't know exactly what she was doing to me.

And when I finally tried to touch her?

She'd slap my hand away. Make me wait.

Then, when I was about to lose my mind, she'd crawl into my lap, free my cock, and sink down onto me, slow and torturous, making me earn it.

The memory alone has my breath hitching.

I lay the nightgown on the bed with one hand, gripping my cock with the other. I stroke myself slowly, the way she would if she were here. I tip my head back, groaning, picturing her in front of me, teasing me.

But it's not enough.

It's not *her*.

It hasn't been her the last fifty times I've come. And that just pisses me off more. With a growl, I grab the bottle of coconut-scented lotion from her nightstand. I pump some into my hand, slicking my length, my breath stuttering at the sensation.

It's closer—between the scent and the slickness, I can almost pretend.

I close my eyes, gripping myself tighter, imagining bending her over the bed.

I'd lift one of her knees, push her upper body down onto the mattress. She'd already be so wet, pushing back against me, eager. She'd reach down, stroking her clit, desperate for release.

Fuck.

I squeeze my cock harder, working my length faster.

She'd be close. She'd work herself harder. And when she shattered, she'd reach back, cupping my balls, pushing herself back onto me, milking every last drop from me.

My groans fill the empty room as I spill onto the nightgown, thick ropes of cum staining the fabric. A dark, satisfied smirk pulls at my lips.

I wish she were here. I'd make her wear it just like this. Make her see how much I still need her.

The thought should be unsettling, but it's not. I shake my head, forcing myself to clear my mind. With a deep breath, I step into the shower, hoping to wash away the frustration clinging to me. But the whole time, my thoughts are still on that damn nightgown.

When I get out, a twisted smile forms, the thought of me leaving it out like that is oddly satisfying. I tell myself I'll wash it later. But I know I won't.

Not yet.

I force myself into work mode, sitting at my desk to prepare for a lunch meeting. Zack, my coworker, set it up, but he didn't give me many details, so I pull together a rundown of our services.

A quick glance at the clock tells me if I don't leave now, I'll be late.

I drive across town, arriving with just enough time to check my reflection.

My tie is slightly crooked, so I adjust it. My hair is a little messier than usual from running my hands through it, but there's nothing I can do about that. I button my navy-blue suit jacket, pick up my briefcase, and head inside.

The hostess tells me my client hasn't arrived yet, so I sit, mentally running through my pitch.

When I glance toward the door, I see a woman with long red hair smiling in my direction.

She's wearing a navy pencil skirt and a matching blouse with a cream-colored blazer. She walks up to the table, and I stand to shake her hand.

"I'm so sorry I'm late," she says, smiling warmly. "I had trouble getting out of the office. I'm Miranda."

"Brian. And it's no problem; I just got here myself."

We sit, both glancing at the menus.

"Have you been here before?" she asks.

"No, have you?"

"Just once. On a date. Obviously, it didn't end well." She laughs lightly.

"Okay, so Zack didn't give me much info. I put together a rundown if you'd like to see it." I reach for my briefcase. I swear I hear her mutter Type A, but I ignore it. "What type of service are you looking for?" I ask.

She chokes on her water, nearly spitting it out.

"Services?" she repeats, dabbing at her lips. "Zack told me you loved your job. But what exactly do you do?"

My brow furrows. "I'm a market researcher. You are a potential client... aren't you?"

She rolls her eyes. "Such a Zack thing to do. No, I'm not a client. I was under the impression this was a date."

My jaw drops.

That son of a bitch.

My fists clench, but she beats me to the frustration.

"You're married?" Her nose scrunches. "Why would he set me up with you?"

"Because he thinks it's time for me to move on."

She studies me. "But you don't want to."

"No."

I don't know why, but I tell her everything. She listens. And when I finish, she hands me a business card.

Dr. Blair Parker, Marriage Counselor.

I look back at her, and she gives me a small, sad smile.

"I see why Zack thought we'd hit it off," she says. "I went through a divorce last year, and my guess is he figured you'd understand me. But I can tell your marriage isn't over—at least not for you. You love your wife very much, and I'm sure she knows it. If she heard the way you talk about her, she wouldn't have any doubts. Talk to her. Tell her what you told me. And call Dr. Parker. She may be unorthodox, and she couldn't help me, but maybe if I'd found her sooner, she could have."

Her last statement sparks some confusion in me, and I'm suddenly intrigued to know more about those *unorthodox* methods.

"Good luck, Brian," she whispers with compassion, getting up to leave.

In the wake of our conversation, for the first time in months, I feel something other than despair.

Hope.

I can't just sit back anymore. It's time to fight for my marriage.

Chapter 6

Erica

The last four months have been so damn hard.

Necessary, but hard.

I miss Brian. God, I miss him. But I've done what I set out to do—find myself. And in doing so, I'm not sure our marriage can be saved. I never want to resent him. I never want him to resent me. But if things keep going the way they were, it's bound to happen.

I've talked to my sister a lot during this time. Maggie always has something to say, but most of it I've ignored. Except for one thing.

One thing I can't ignore.

"How do you know Brian hasn't been seeing someone else since you left?"

At the time, I scoffed. Because he loves me. Because I know him.

But now?

Now, that question has burrowed its way into my brain, sinking deep, taking root. Which is why I'm standing in front of the mirror, staring at my reflection.

My blonde hair is pulled into a simple ponytail, brushing the nape of my neck. The olive-green crewneck dress I picked clings to my torso but flows loosely from my waist down, grazing just past my knees. Cream-colored flats complete the look, along with a small silver necklace.

Satisfied, I grab my phone, checking for messages.

Greg texted ten minutes ago—he's almost here.

Greg is a vendor at the farmer's market. I met him early on when I first started going with my mom. He was easy to talk to, easy to be around. And from the moment Maggie noticed him sneaking glances at me, she's been determined to push us together. He's asked me out a couple of times, and I've politely declined. He knows I'm still married and respects that.

Tonight isn't a date.

It's dinner.

Dinner to get Maggie off my back.

If I'm being honest, he seems more interested in her anyway. But when he was invited to partner with a restaurant as a vegetable vendor, he asked me to join him for a meal to check the place out.

I agreed.

Now, standing in front of the mirror, I wonder if that was a mistake.

I grab my jacket, tuck my things into my purse, and head downstairs. As I reach the last few steps, I spot Maggie at the front door, talking to Greg. Or rather, *flirting* with Greg.

His attention is entirely on her, and she's soaking it up. She must have been in the sunroom doing yoga when he arrived—her lavender yoga pants and black t-shirt are proof enough of that. It also explains why I didn't hear the doorbell.

I take the opportunity to study him.

Greg looks good tonight—clean, simple, put together. He's dressed in a light blue button-down, the sleeves rolled up, tucked into dark blue jeans. A pair of well-worn boots complete the look. His dark red hair is styled forward, though the front is brushed up slightly at an angle. Neither of them notices me until I reach the bottom step and stub my toe.

"Shit!"

The curse makes Maggie whip her head toward me, her expression almost annoyed.

I roll my eyes. *This was your idea, remember?* Ignoring her, I turn my attention to Greg. "Are you ready?"

Maggie steps aside with a tight-lipped smile, but I catch the look in her eyes before she shuts the door, barely missing my ass.

Oh, *now* I have a plan. If I have to suffer through this dinner, she does too.

Greg shakes his head slightly, offering me his arm. "Sure."

As we step outside, I glance at him. "So, are you excited about the new partnership with the restaurant?"

"Yeah," he nods, leading me to his truck.

That's all I get. One word.

The old Chevy has definitely seen better days, but he steps aside, opening the door for me.

"Thanks."

He barely acknowledges it, walking around to the driver's side and climbing in.

The ride is quiet. Uncomfortably so. The only thing breaking the silence is the radio, which I silently thank him for turning on.

This is not like him. If my suspicions are correct, it has everything to do with the strawberry-blonde we just left behind.

I pull out my phone, preparing a quick message to Maggie.

> Hey, I need you to do me a favor. No questions asked. Get dressed and get your sorry ass to Ian's Bar & Grill. I can't do this, and I can't just ditch Greg.

I hit send, then turn my attention back to him.

"Greg, is everything okay?" I reach over, placing a hand on his shoulder, pulling him out of his thoughts.

He exhales, shaking his head slightly. "Yeah, I'm okay."

He's not okay.

That sigh? I know that sigh. I've let out a dozen just like it. It's laced with longing.

"It's just that..." he hesitates, then shakes his head. "You know what? It's not important."

Oh, Greg.

I sit quietly for the rest of the drive, knowing I shouldn't be the one celebrating with him tonight.

My phone buzzes.

> **Are you sure?**

> Yes. I have the feeling I'm not the sister he wants here tonight. What the hell did you say to him?

> **I'm so sorry. I just told him I left Dipshit for good, and it's been over for a couple of months. He said our timing was never right, and then you tripped like the klutz you are, and that was it.**

Jesus, Maggie.

> Well, hurry up. I'll order you a veggie burger with fries. Let me know when you get here.

> I owe you one.

I smirk, tucking my phone away just as Greg pulls into the parking lot. He gets out without saying a word and walks around to open my door.

By the time we get inside and find a table, twenty minutes have passed. Still no word from Maggie. I stall, telling the waitress we need a little longer with the menu. When she walks away, I look across the table at Greg and smirk. Might as well get this over with.

"I hope you know I only agreed to this date to get my sister to shut up."

Greg nearly spits out the water he just took a sip of.

"Oh?" he coughs, setting the glass down on the wooden tabletop.

"Mhm," I nod. "In fact, I planned to enjoy your company as a friend. And if you asked for a second date, I would have politely declined, saying, 'It's not the right time in my life; I need to focus on myself and figure out my marriage.' I'd let you down easy."

Even though the words are meant as a joke, they hit harder than I expect—because I realize that's exactly what I told Brian.

Greg exhales, his shoulders visibly relaxing. So he hadn't expected this to be a real date either.

"What is going on with your marriage?" he asks carefully. "You don't have to tell me if you don't want to."

I sigh. If he's going to date my sister, he'll know sooner or later.

"Brian and I hit a rough patch. We've been trying to get pregnant for almost a year." My voice drops slightly. "I was afraid that if we went to a clinic and found out I was the problem, he'd start to resent me. And then I'd resent him. I left because I hadn't felt like me in a while. I wasn't in the right mindset to take the next step."

I fight back the stinging behind my eyes.

"Does he know how you were feeling?"

I shake my head just as the waitress comes back. We place our orders, and I glance at my phone—Maggie will be here in twenty minutes.

"So does he?" Greg presses.

"No. I just left to think. To be me without the pressure." A self-deprecating scoff escapes me. "The funny thing is, about two months before I left, he suggested we stop trying. I got so mad. I felt like he was giving up on me. I didn't talk to him for a week. And then, when I started ovulating, I became even more determined, and it just consumed me. I never really gave him a chance to explain why he suggested it in the first place. So I guess... I ran."

A single tear slips down my cheek.

I ran.

And for the first time, it hits me—I never gave Brian a chance to process his emotions. I never considered what he was going through.

My breath catches in my throat.

"Do you want to know what I think?" Greg asks, squeezing my hand gently.

I nod.

"Good, because I was going to tell you anyway," he smirks before his expression softens. "I think he loves you. And when he suggested taking a break from trying, it was only to take the pressure off of you. If he really loves you, he'd be open to other options—adoption, surrogacy, anything—because all that would matter is *you*. Being parents *together*."

How had I only focused on the bad? How had I never thought of it that way?

"Probably because you were depressed and couldn't," Greg shrugs.

I blink. I hadn't meant to say that aloud. But he's right. I was depressed.

And I need to talk to Brian.

I check my phone—Maggie will be here in a couple of minutes.

I turn my gaze back to Greg, smiling softly. "Since you gave me such good advice, I'm going to return the favor."

"Oh?" he raises a brow. "I don't really need relationship advice. I'm not in one."

I don't miss the way his fingers tighten around his water glass or the way his eyes flick toward the waitress as he flags her down.

"Whiskey and ginger ale, with a lime."

I cover my laugh with a cough.

"Make that two."

His eyebrows shoot up.

"What? I know someone who drinks that all the time." I smirk.

"Who?"

"Maggie. *No caffeine that late*, she says."

His lips part slightly, but no words come out.

"Now, as for your relationship advice," I tease. "Let me tell you something you might not know—sometimes, people are over a relationship before they actually leave. And sometimes, they're over someone before they even realize it."

Greg furrows his brows. "I don't follow."

"Maggie has been over her ex for a long time. She just didn't realize it. The only reason she stayed was because she felt like she had to—like she owed it to Mike to keep trying. But really, they'd grown apart.

Neither of them wanted to hurt each other. And then..." I pause, giving him a knowing look. "She found him in bed with someone else."

The gears are turning in his head.

"Greg, you like my sister, right?"

His cheeks redden as he rubs the back of his neck.

"The timing has never been right."

"Well, I can tell you Maggie likes you too."

I glance past him, spotting her standing near the hostess stand, shifting nervously.

"Did she tell you that?" His voice is careful, but there's hope in his eyes.

"She didn't have to. I saw it. And that's why I have to leave now." I push back from the table, grabbing my purse. "Enjoy your date."

Greg looks over his shoulder just as Maggie spots us.

She's changed into boot-cut jeans and a white tank top, her strawberry-blonde hair brushing just past her shoulders. Greg exhales slowly, eyes locked on her.

"I texted Maggie on the way here," I admit, grabbing my jacket. "I could tell she was the one you wanted here tonight. And I've been around my sister long enough to know when she's into someone. It just took her longer to realize it."

Greg stares at me, stunned.

"Don't worry about taking me home—she drove, so I'll take her car."

I step around him, heading for Maggie.

"I need your keys, Maggs," I say, snapping my fingers in her face to break her out of whatever trance she and Greg just fell into.

"What? Oh. Yeah, here." She finally looks at me, digging into her purse and dropping her keys into my palm. Then, without warning, she wraps her arms around me, hugging me tightly.

"Thank you." Her voice is soft, almost shaky.

I squeeze her back. "No, thank you."

She pulls back, brows furrowed. "For what?"

I take her hands in mine. "I hadn't realized I needed to talk to Brian until tonight. If you hadn't pushed me to do this, I don't know when I would have figured it out."

Her lips part, her eyes searching mine.

"I'm going home tomorrow. I have to pack."

Her face splits into a grin. "You're going home?"

I nod. "I'm going home to my husband."

She beams, and I kiss her cheek before turning toward the exit. I have a lot to do. Because tomorrow, I'm going back where I belong.

Chapter 7

Brian

By the time I leave the restaurant, it's close to four. I had called the office to let them know I wouldn't be in the rest of the day. I couldn't be in. Not when my mind was consumed with her.

The second I get home, I waste no time changing out of my work clothes. Black t-shirt. Faded jeans. Then I throw some clothes into a bag. I'll book a hotel room once I'm on the road—I don't want to waste a single second. The drive is only about three hours. If I push it, I can be there by eight. For the first time in months, I feel like I'm doing something right. Like I'm fighting for her.

For us.

But with less than an hour left in my drive, my gas light comes on.

Shit.

I keep an eye out for the next station and find one five miles up the road. I pull into the lot, filling up the tank while I call to book my hotel. With that settled, I continue the drive, anticipation building with every passing mile.

When I finally pull into her parents' driveway, something unexpected hits me.

Nerves.

I haven't spoken to her in four months.

What if she doesn't want to see me?

What if I'm too late?

I take a deep breath, get out of the car, and make my way up the sidewalk. My fist hovers over the bright yellow door for only a moment before I knock.

When the door opens, I come face-to-face with her mother, surprise filling her features.

"Brian, Erica didn't say you were stopping by."

I rake a hand through my hair, exhaling slowly. "She doesn't know. I need to talk to her, Nina. Please."

Her lips press into a thin line, hesitation clear in her expression.

"I'm sorry, she's not here right now. I'll let her know you stopped by when she comes back."

She's not here? My stomach twists. Where is she?

"Is it okay if I just wait for her?" My voice is thick, almost desperate. "It's really important I see her."

Nina sighs, stepping onto the porch and shutting the door behind her. She moves to the porch swing, patting the spot beside her.

"Take a seat, Brian."

I do, bile threatening to climb up my throat at her expression.

She inhales deeply, before she carefully says, "Brian, she's on a date."

I stop breathing.

She's on a *date*?

"What?" My face drops into my hands as a sharp pain lances through my chest.

"Maggie set her up with a vendor from the farmers' market," Nina explains softly. "I was surprised when she agreed, but... here we are."

I barely hear her. My ears are ringing, my head spinning. Did I come all this way just to realize I was too late?

The sound of gravel crunching under tires makes me snap my head up.

"It's just Maggie," Nina says.

I drop my head again, my heart hammering. The sound of a car door shutting, footsteps on the walkway. Then, a sharp intake of breath.

"Brian?"

My head jerks up so fast I almost get whiplash.

She's here.

She's standing right in front of me.

"What are you doing here?" she asks.

I try to speak, but the words won't come.

I just stare.

She looks... beautiful.

Her green knee-length dress hugs her body in a way that makes my fingers twitch to touch her. To hold her. To make sure she's real.

"Where's Maggie?" Nina asks.

But I can't focus on anything except her.

"She's with Greg," Erica says softly, her gaze locked onto mine.

Nina frowns. "I thought you were on a date with him?"

Erica swallows hard. "I was. But I only went to get Maggie off my case. And when I saw how they were looking at each other, I told her to take my place."

She left the date.

She didn't want to be there.

Before I can stop myself, I'm standing. Moving toward her. Closing the distance in just a few strides. I reach up, cupping her face between my hands, tilting her chin so she has to look at me.

"I see. Well, I'll leave you two to talk," Nina says, retreating into the house.

But I barely hear her.

Because Erica is *right here*.

I can feel her breath against my lips.

Her eyes are shining, emotions swirling in their deep blue depths.

"Brian, I—"

I cut her off with a kiss.

For a moment, she stiffens, her hands pressing against my chest as if to push me away. But then she fists my shirt, pulling me closer. She brushes her tongue along the seam of my lips, and I gladly part for her, deepening the kiss, pouring everything I can't say into the way my lips move against hers.

I step forward, pressing her against the wooden post of the porch, molding my body to hers. She gasps when she feels how hard I am for her, and a soft moan escapes her lips.

I need more.

But before I can take things further, she pulls back, panting. Her eyes flick to mine, glassy with unshed tears. "Brian, I am so sorry."

A single tear slips free, and before I can wipe it away, she buries her face against my chest and sobs. I wrap my arms around her, holding her tightly, kissing the top of her head.

"Erica, love. I understand." I inhale deeply, grounding myself in her scent. "I won't say I'm not hurt that you left, because I am. I won't say I forgive you, because I'm not there yet. But I understand."

She looks up at me through wet lashes, a small smile forming. "I've missed you so much," she whispers.

"Me too."

"I know we need to talk," she says hesitantly. "But I don't want to do it here. Let's go to the diner."

I simply nod in agreement. Anything for her.

Without hesitation, I grab her hand and start leading her toward my car.

But she stops me. "I need to tell my mom first. I'll meet you there."

I nod again, reluctantly releasing her hand.

As I wait by my car, I remind myself—she was on a date, but she left.

She's here with me.

That's what matters.

When she finally walks toward me, I open her door, reaching for her.

But before she can climb inside, I press her against the side of the car, burying my face in her neck. She shudders as my nose grazes her skin, my lips brushing her ear.

"We can talk later," I murmur, pressing against her, groaning at the friction. "Right now, I need you."

Her fingers dig into my forearms, like she'd melt if I let her go. I pull back slightly, searching her face, looking for any hesitation.

But all I see is desire.

Her pupils are blown. Her breath is ragged. And when she gives a slight nod, heat surges through me. She climbs into the car, and I shut the door before making my way around. When we're both buckled, I start the engine, the silence between us charged. We don't speak as I pull onto the road. Because right now, there's nothing left to say.

We've both made our choice.

And the second I get her alone, I'm going to show her *exactly* what that means.

Chapter 8

Erica

The tension between Brian and me is thick, suffocating.

He grips the steering wheel tightly, his knuckles white. His whole body radiates need—not just desire, but *need*. The kind that settles deep in your bones, the kind that makes you ache.

And I feel it too.

I hadn't realized just how much I needed him until tonight.

Glancing over at him, my pulse thrumming. There's something about him right now—the way he's holding himself, the heat in his gaze—that reminds me of the first time we ever made love.

And with that thought, I'm lost in the memory.

We've been together for six months.

It's Oliver's wedding—Brian's best friend. One of Oliver's brothers, Tim, has been hitting on me relentlessly since the rehearsal dinner. And at the wedding, he takes the open seat beside me, using every opportunity to provoke Brian.

I know exactly what he's doing. So, to shut him up, I agree to one dance.

"One dance," I tell him. "And after that, you'll see exactly why I won't be leaving with you."

He laughs, confident. Cocky.

But by the time the song ends, I'm still smiling—not because of him, but because of Brian, who's watching from across the room.

Tim dips me unexpectedly, and I laugh. When I walk away, I don't have to turn around to know Brian is tense, his jaw locked.

And when I do look at him? It does something to me.

His hair is slightly disheveled, his tie loosened, a few buttons of his dress shirt undone. His sleeves rolled up, exposing the veins along his forearms. His black slacks fitted perfectly, outlining the strong muscles of his thighs.

He looks *sinfully* good.

I walk straight up to him, grab his loosened tie, and pull him in for a kiss.

A kiss that isn't soft.

It's *possessive*.

He takes my mouth, pulling me into him almost roughly, his fingers threading into my hair, tugging just enough to make me gasp. And he takes advantage of that gasp, sliding his tongue against mine, claiming every inch of me in a way he never has outside the bedroom. When he finally pulls away, his forehead rests against mine, both of us breathless.

Then his gaze flicks over my shoulder, and he smirks—the kind of smirk that tells me Tim has just gotten the message loud and clear.

He leans in, voice rough.

"The bride and groom snuck off. Why don't we head up to our room?"

All I can do is nod.

He takes my hand, pulling me through the ballroom, straight into the elevator.

The second we step into our hotel room, the door has barely clicked shut before I'm against it.

His hands are everywhere.

His teeth nip at my neck, at my collarbone, his fingers tracing over my curves. My breath comes in short gasps, my head spinning from how badly I want him—how badly I *need* him. Then he drops to his knees, taking off my flats. Once they're gone, he doesn't stand right away. Instead, his hands trail up my calves, up my thighs, pushing the fabric of my floor-length burgundy dress higher and higher.

"Did you enjoy making me jealous?" His voice is low, dangerous. Threatening.

So *that's* what this is about.

"I wasn't trying to make you jealous." My voice trembles with need.

"Weren't you?" His lips skim the delicate skin of my thigh, a phantom touch that sends a shiver racing up my spine. "And what exactly did he promise you?" His voice is a low, dangerous drawl, the kind that makes my breath hitch. "Did he tell you he could take better care of you than I could?"

I nod, deliberately slow, letting the confession drip from my lips like honey. "He said he could give me things. Do things you never would."

The flicker in Brian's eyes shifts into something darker, something primal. Possessiveness wraps around him like a second skin, and it is *intoxicating*. I never thought jealousy would look this good on a man—but Brian, undone by it, is something else entirely. And God help me, I want to push him further.

His grip tightens, his breath hot against my skin. And then, just as I thought I won this game, Brian tilts his head, smirks, and whispers, "Is that what you think, sweetheart?"

Instead of answering, I just continue pushing his buttons. I need to unravel him completely. "He said he could please me in ways you never would know how to."

The words have barely left my lips before he acts. His fingers tear my thong to the side, thrusting two fingers inside of me so fast and deep that the air escapes my lungs.

"That doesn't sound like you really believe that." His voice is a low, heated rasp as his thumb finds my clit, and at the same moment, his mouth latches onto my nipple through my dress. His touch is relentless—his hands, his mouth—tearing me apart, unraveling me in record time.

"I don't think I could ever get enough of you like this." His words are a dark promise as he spins me around, pressing me flush against the door. I glance over my shoulder, only to find him right there—eyes ablaze, mouth stealing mine in a kiss that's all heat and need. The moment my dress pools at my feet, Brian wastes no time, dragging me to the bed.

He lays me out, and the way he looks at me—like I'm something to be worshiped—has my body clenching around nothing. He crawls over me, lips brushing mine before he kisses his way down, leaving a trail of fire in his wake. The little touches, the reverent caresses, make me feel so cherished I almost want to cry.

"I still don't think you understand that no man will ever make you feel the way I do." His words barely register before a moan rips from my throat—Brian's tongue sweeps across me, teasing, tasting, before he sucks my clit into his mouth. Then, as if he's been waiting to ruin me, he pushes two fingers inside, curling them perfectly to find my g-spot. My back arches, but his other hand presses down on my stomach, holding me in place as his mouth and fingers work in devastating tandem.

Everything fades except for him—his touch, his tongue, the way every nerve in my body hums with the oncoming wave of pleasure. It builds, higher and higher, until I shatter. My fingers clutch at the sheets, but Brian doesn't let up. If anything, he sucks my clit harder, flicks his tongue faster, pumps his fingers deeper. My thighs tremble, my breath catches, and I lose myself again—gasping for air, drowning in him.

Somehow, my fingers find his hair, and I tug hard, pulling him up my body, dragging his mouth back to mine. The taste of myself on his lips makes me moan, and when I grind against him, his cock—still restrained by his pants—presses hot and thick against my thigh.

"Let me taste you now." I don't even recognize my own voice—it's breathless, desperate. I make quick work of his shirt, and as soon as I push it off, Brian takes my nipple into his mouth, scraping his teeth over the sensitive bud.

My back bows into him, pleasure coursing through me like fire, and he smirks. "You can't possibly think he could please you better."

I shake my head no, reaching for his pants, and he doesn't make me wait. He shoves them down, along with his boxers, and the moment he's bare, I push him onto his back. I want control now. He doesn't resist, and that pleases me to no end.

I trail kisses down his chest, over his stomach, before I finally take him into my mouth, swirling my tongue around his tip, savoring the taste of him. He groans—a deep, primal sound—his hips bucking as I take him deeper.

"You can't possibly think I'd want anyone but you." My words are a whisper before I swallow him down again, letting him hit the back of my throat.

I don't really know what to think after that dance, but I know I don't want you to stop what you're doing now," he groans, dropping his head back on the pillow.

I situate myself between his legs, laying on my stomach to get comfortable. "Eyes on me; watch what I do to you," I whisper, and he immediately props up on his elbows, his gaze hot on mine.

I lick him from base to tip, swirling my tongue around the head before taking him even deeper, cheeks hollowed for more suction.

"Fuck, you look so sexy like that," he groans, and I moan around his cock in response, making it jerk in my mouth. I take him deeper with every descent of my head, his sounds encouraging me for more.

Brian's control snaps. His fingers tangle in my hair, pulling me off him just before he flips me onto my back and pins me beneath him. "That's enough teasing for tonight. I think you've done plenty already, don't you?" His smirk is wicked, but the way he reaches for the bedside table—the foil wrapper—tells me exactly how much restraint he's barely holding onto.

For a moment, I find my voice. "Brian... are you sure? We don't have to. I'm happy with how things are."

He settles between my legs, his cock pressing against my entrance. "And that right there is why I love you." His voice is steady but laced with something deeper—something raw. "You never push me. You never expect more than I'm willing to give. And I've never wanted this... not until you. Others tried, but I just wasn't interested. But tonight? After everything?" His thumb brushes over my cheek, his gaze dark and unyielding. "I need to make you mine in every sense of the word—if you'll let me."

My breath catches. He just told me he loves me.

Who said this wasn't romantic? Because right now, nothing in the world feels more perfect than being wanted—claimed—like this.

"I love you too, Brian. I'm yours."

The second the words leave my lips, he thrusts into me. A sharp gasp escapes me—a perfect mix of pain and pleasure.

"Shit, baby. You're so tight... fuck, I won't last long." His jaw clenches, his muscles taut as he fights for control. I pull him down, kiss him slow and deep, and he finds a rhythm—one that has me clinging to him, nails scraping down his back as he drives me higher.

Before he can finish, he pulls out abruptly, flipping me onto my hands and knees. His palm presses firmly against my back, urging my chest lower, and I shudder as his lips graze my spine—a teasing contrast to the way he dominates my body.

Then he thrusts into me again, deep and unrelenting. A cry rips from my throat as he finds that devastating spot inside me, the one that has me unraveling with every stroke. He knows exactly what he's doing. His hand snakes around, fingers finding my clit, rubbing in slow, merciless circles.

I see stars.

"Come for me again, baby. I want to feel it."

His voice is dark, possessive, and when he pinches my clit, it's all I need. My body clenches around him, gripping him tight as pleasure crashes through me, wave after wave, dragging him deeper into my madness. His thrusts falter, slowing—but I'm not done with him yet.

"My turn."

Before he can move me again, I grab his arm, pulling him onto the bed. He barely has time to catch his breath before I straddle his waist, taking control. Holding his gaze, I reach between us, guiding him to where I need him most.

And then, slowly, I sink down onto him.

Every inch stretches me, fills me, until we're flush—pelvis to pelvis—my swollen walls molding to him like we were made for this. His jaw tightens, his hands gripping my thighs as I roll my hips, grinding against him, making him hit that spot deep inside me over and over.

His eyes stay locked on where we're joined, dark and hungry. I take his hand and press it to my lower stomach.

"Feel that?" I whisper. "That's you inside me."

A groan tears from his lips, but he doesn't move his hand.

"Use your thumb—rub my clit." My voice is a breathy demand.

He obeys without hesitation. The second his thumb finds that sensitive bundle of nerves, pleasure surges through me, making my walls flutter around him. My head falls back as I ride him harder, faster.

"Fuck," he grits out. "I'm so close."

His control shatters. He thrusts up to meet me, hips snapping, grunts turning to low, desperate groans. The friction, the pressure, the heat—it's too much.

And then we break together, bodies locking, gasps and moans tangled as we come undone, lost in each other.

"Erica, baby... we're here."

I blink, clearing the haze of memories clouding my mind. The car has stopped in front of the hotel, city lights casting a soft glow against the windows.

"Oh."

I'm so wound up from thinking about that night—our night. Everything about Brian tonight reminds me of him then. The same smoldering intensity in his eyes, the quiet possessiveness in his touch.

His voice pulls me back. "We don't have to... we can just talk if you'd rather—"

"No," I cut in quickly. "It's not that." I hesitate, swallowing hard. "I was just thinking about our first time together."

A flicker of something dark, something knowing, crosses his face. He reaches over, his thumb tracing the curve of my lips. "And what about that night?" His voice is softer now, laced with something deeper.

I glance down, wringing my hands together before forcing myself to meet his gaze. "I see the same fire in you tonight that I did then."

He chuckles, low and rough. "Is that so?"

I nod, and his thumb tugs my bottom lip down, teasing, testing.

"I've missed you, Brian." My voice is barely above a whisper, but I know he hears it.

He leans in, his lips brushing mine, featherlight. "Then let's head up, shall we?"

He starts to pull away, but I've missed him too damn much. Before I can stop myself, my hand tangles in the back of his neck, dragging him back to me. Our mouths collide in a kiss that's anything but gentle. It's desperate, aching, filled with every bottled-up emotion I can't put into words.

Brian groans against my lips before pulling away just enough to catch his breath. His hand wraps around mine, firm, insistent.

"Come on," he murmurs, and then we're moving—through the hotel lobby, past curious glances, and into the elevator, where the real unraveling begins.

Chapter 9

BRIAN

The elevator doors slide shut, and all I want to do is pull Erica to me and claim her mouth again—devour her, consume her. But a family stands beside us, two small children wrapped in damp towels, their hair dripping from the pool. So, I clench my fists and swallow down the frustration, the hunger.

The ride is mercifully short. As soon as we step into the hallway, I grab her hand, leading her to my room. My fingers twitch around the keycard, and it feels like a goddamn eternity before the lock finally clicks open.

The moment we step inside, the air thickens, charged with something raw and electric. I reach for the door, sliding the *Do Not Disturb* sign in place before locking it. When I turn back, Erica stands in the center of the room, watching me.

I see it—the hesitation, the words hovering on the tip of her tongue. But I don't want words right now. Words can wait.

I need *her*.

She must see it written all over my face. She always could read me better than anyone. Her gaze drags over me, pausing at my waistband where my aching cock strains against the fabric. It's been this way since we were at her parents' house. Hell, I had to tuck it up in my jeans just to make it through the hotel lobby.

Then she does it—her tongue darts out, grazing her bottom lip.

I snap. No—*we* snap.

We crash together, a collision of heat, teeth, hands. Her dress disappears over her head, my shirt yanked off in turn, and our lips barely part long enough to shed the last barriers between us. Her hands slide down my torso, fingers teasing over my abs before reaching my waistband.

She doesn't hesitate. She unbuttons my jeans, slipping her soft hand inside my boxers, fingers wrapping around my cock. I groan at the contact, my head tilting back as she strokes me—slow, teasing, devastating.

I retaliate.

With her bra already discarded, I dip my head, catching her nipple between my lips. I flick my tongue over it, then bite down just enough to make her gasp. She arches into me, and I move to the other breast, giving it the same sweet torment.

My hands skim down her body, tracing the curves I know too damn well—the dip of her waist, the flare of her hips. Then, I find what I want.

My fingers slide between her thighs, pressing against the damp lace of her panties. She's soaking for me. I suck hard on her nipple, and at the same time, my thumb finds her clit, rubbing slow, tight circles. She whimpers, her head tipping back, giving me full access to her throat.

I turn her around, kissing my way down her spine, feeling the shivers beneath my lips. When I reach her ass, I bite down lightly, making her yelp. Then I hook my fingers into her dark brown panties, dragging them down her legs.

"Step out," I murmur. She does, and I guide her toward the desk, positioning her in front of the mirror above it. "Put your hands on the desk."

She obeys, and I take a moment to look—to admire the reflection of the woman I've craved every damn night since she left. Her flushed cheeks, her parted lips, the curves of her body that haunt my every thought.

When our eyes meet in the mirror, I step closer, brushing my lips over her shoulder, the back of her neck. Then, I trail my tongue down her spine, savoring the way her body shudders under my mouth.

She moans, soft and breathy.

I drop to my knees behind her, spreading her open with my hands.

Then I *feast*.

My tongue swipes over her slit, slow and deliberate, before I bury it deep inside her. She jolts, her hands gripping the desk as I work her with my mouth, sucking, licking, fucking her with my tongue. Her moans break apart into desperate little cries, her body trembling as she gets closer.

When she starts to tighten around me, I shift my attention to her clit. I flick my tongue over the swollen bud, sucking hard, refusing to let up even as she squirms.

"Brian—fuck, please—"

Only when her thighs begin to shake violently do I pull away. I stand behind her, and the sight of her—cheeks flushed, lips swollen, pupils blown with desire—has my restraint snapping like a frayed wire.

I don't wait.

I grab my cock, line it up with her dripping pussy, and thrust inside in one hard, deep stroke.

"Fuck—" I groan, head tipping back.

Her tight heat grips me like a vice, squeezing me so perfectly I almost lose myself right then.

"I've needed you so damn bad," I growl, thrusting hard. "These last few months, I couldn't satisfy myself. I needed you. This tight, wet pussy. No one else."

Her moan is wrecked. "I missed you, Brian—"

I smack her ass, and she gasps, pushing back against me, silently begging for more.

"You broke my fucking heart when you left me." Another slap, this one harder. Her body jolts, but her moan is pure pleasure.

"I'm sorry—" she chokes out between gasps.

I pull out abruptly, my chest heaving, my fingers digging into her hips. "And then I come back to find out you were on a date?" My voice is sharp, edged with something dark.

I scoff, about to lift her onto the desk, but before I can—she drops to her knees.

"I didn't do it to get over you," she says, looking up at me with wide, desperate eyes. "I could never get over you."

Then she takes me into her mouth.

My head snaps back, a guttural groan tearing from my throat. Her tongue swirls around the tip before she hollows her cheeks, sucking hard. Just as my fingers reach for her hair, she pulls back, her lips glistening, her gaze locked on mine.

"Let me show you how sorry I am," she murmurs, rising slowly, her breasts brushing over my stomach on her way up.

"How?" My voice is rough, barely human.

"Lay back on the bed."

I don't argue.

I strip off the last of my clothes and collapse onto the mattress, my legs spread, waiting. She climbs on top of me, her milky-white thighs straddling my hips.

She grips my cock, rubbing it over her clit, teasing herself before she sinks down—inch by torturous inch—until she takes all of me.

I groan, reaching for her, but she stops me, pressing my hands to the mattress.

"I said let me show you," she whispers against my ear. "Now *let me*."

Then she moves.

Rolling her hips, grinding down, working me with slow, devastating strokes. Her moans are filthy, her head tilting back as she rides me harder, faster.

"Fuck, baby—" I grit my teeth, my spine arching as pleasure coils tight, ready to snap. "If you don't stop, I won't last—"

Her smirk is lethal. She bounces faster, rocking harder.

"Let me touch you, please," I rasp, desperate.

She releases my hands, and I move instantly—gripping her breast, squeezing her hip. My body tenses, the sharp pleasure cresting—

Then I'm gone.

I explode inside her, groaning her name as she clenches around me, her own release crashing into her. My vision whites out as I thrust twice more, wringing every last drop I have to give her.

When it's over, she collapses on top of me, her body still shuddering with aftershocks.

I kiss her forehead, then move to stand. "Let me clean you up."

She stops me, her fingers curling around my wrist.

"Let's take a shower instead."

She's stalling. Avoiding the conversation that's bound to come.

But I let her.

For now.

Chapter 10

Erica

As I stare at my reflection in the dim hotel bathroom, a strange sensation washes over me—peace. For the first time in months, I feel whole again. Being here, in the presence of my husband, wrapped in the lingering warmth of his touch, I feel like myself. A small, hesitant smile tugs at my lips. How long has it been since I last felt this content? Since I last felt truly desired—not just physically, but deeply, soulfully?

Yet, even as my heart hums with satisfaction, a shadow lingers. The conversation we need to have looms over us like an unspoken storm. I know Brian will be hurt. I know there will be anger. And maybe, just maybe, there will be healing too.

A warm hand on mine pulls me from my thoughts. I look up to find Brian watching me with an unreadable expression, his fingers lacing through mine as he leads me into the shower. It's small, barely made for two, but we make it work, moving around each other in an intimate, silent dance. There's no urgency now—no feverish touches, no desperate need to consume one another. Just slow, reverent hands, washing away months of pain and separation.

Neither of us speaks.

The silence stretches, heavy with unsaid words.

When we finally step out, the reality of what's coming crashes down on me. I have nothing to wear except the clothes I arrived in, a reminder of how temporary I thought this visit would be.

As if reading my mind, Brian clears his throat. "I, uh... had wishful thinking," he admits, rubbing the back of his neck. "Packed you a couple of things."

I turn, eyes falling on a small duffel bag sitting on the bed. My fingers tremble as I unzip it, finding neatly folded clothes—underwear, a soft nightgown, a pair of shorts, and two of his shirts.

He packed for me.

Tears prick my eyes. This isn't just hope—this is faith.

"Thank you," I whisper, my voice thick with emotion.

Turning away, I drop my towel and step into a pair of panties, pulling the nightgown over my head. Before I can process it, a low groan rumbles from behind me. Heat rushes to my cheeks as I glance over my shoulder, catching the way Brian's gaze darkens, locked onto me with a hunger that sends a shiver down my spine.

He takes a step forward, slow and deliberate.

I step back, my body pressing against the cool wall.

"You've been without me for four months," I tease, attempting to lighten the mood. "Surely you've taken care of things."

His jaw tightens, his eyes never leaving mine. "Nothing compares to you." His voice is husky, raw, filled with a need that nearly makes me forget why we need to talk.

Almost.

I place a hand on his chest, feeling the steady drum of his heartbeat beneath my palm. "Bri, we need to talk."

His shoulders sag, and the fire in his gaze dims slightly. But instead of resisting, he presses a kiss to the top of my head and nods. "You're right."

Taking my hand, he leads me to the desk chair. I sink into it, wrapping my arms around myself as I watch him sit at the foot of the bed, elbows resting on his knees, head bowed.

For a long moment, neither of us speaks.

Then, finally, he looks up. "Do you still love me?" His voice is barely above a whisper, as if he's afraid of the answer.

My breath catches.

"What? Of course, I do! How could you ask that?" I push up from my seat, closing the distance between us, kneeling between his legs. I take his hands in mine, forcing him to look at me.

"Bri, I didn't leave because I stopped loving you." My voice trembles, but I press on. "I left because I wasn't happy, and when I tried to talk to you about it, you didn't understand. I needed space—to find myself again, to accept our situation, to figure out why I felt the way I did. I was scared, Brian. Scared that if we stayed the way we were, we'd start resenting each other. And I never, ever wanted to resent you."

I cup his cheek, my thumb brushing against the faint stubble on his jaw.

His eyes search mine, filled with so much pain and longing that it nearly undoes me.

"I was going to pack my bags tonight," I confess, "and come home tomorrow."

Something shifts in his expression—something lighter, something hopeful. He lets out a breath, a ghost of a smile flickering across his lips.

"Okay," he says softly. Then, rubbing the back of his neck, he clears his throat. "I, uh... I have something to tell you."

The hesitance in his voice makes my stomach twist.

"What is it?"

He swallows hard. "I... I sort of had a date today too."

I freeze.

The air between us thickens, sharp and electric.

Slowly, I rise to my feet, my arms crossing over my chest.

"It's not what you think," he rushes out. "Actually... it's kind of a funny story."

I arch a brow. "A funny story?" My voice is dangerously calm. "Do tell me how my husband going on a date with another woman is amusing."

He smirks slightly, his hands resting on his knees. "Are you jealous, baby?"

My jaw clenches. "Just start talking, Brian."

He chuckles, but the humor fades quickly. "Do you remember Zach? The guy I work with?"

I nod, still glaring.

"He set me up with his cousin. Told me it was a business meeting—I even prepped a whole pitch for a potential contract."

Despite myself, I blink. "Wait... what?"

Brian grins now, shaking his head. "Yeah. She thought it was a date, but we got to talking, and somehow, we ended up talking about you. She's the one who gave me the name of a marriage counselor."

My heart stutters.

"I came here tonight," he continues, "to ask if you'd be willing to go with me. To fight for us. I already called her office—I made an appointment for tomorrow at one."

Tears blur my vision.

"You came here for me?" I whisper. "To take me to marriage counseling? To save us?"

Brian reaches up, wiping away a stray tear with his thumb. "Of course, I did. I tried to give you space, but baby... I need you. I'm not me without you."

I can't hold back anymore.

I crash into him, my lips finding his in a kiss filled with every emotion I can't put into words.

It doesn't turn into more than that—just deep, lingering kisses, filled with promises and unspoken vows.

Tomorrow, we'll pack my bags. Tomorrow, we'll start fighting for our marriage.

For the first time in months, I fall asleep easily, wrapped in the warmth of Brian's arms.

For the first time in months, I have hope.

Chapter 11

Brian

We woke up tangled in each other's arms, warm and sated, the sheets still infused with the remnants of the night before. For the first time in months, there had been no hesitance in our touches, no uncertainty in our gazes—just the quiet, unspoken understanding that we were finally where we belonged.

After we pulled ourselves from the cocoon of blankets and skin, we went to breakfast at the old diner we used to love—the kind of place where the coffee is always fresh, the pancakes are always stacked high, and the smell of sizzling bacon lingers in the air like an old friend.

And we simply…talked.

Really talked.

It wasn't about trying or failing, about leaving or hurting. It was just us—Brian and Erica—the way we used to be, the way I had missed us being.

It felt almost *normal*—the clatter of plates, the scent of fresh coffee, the murmur of conversation around us. We talked, nothing too heavy, just the kind of easy, natural conversation we hadn't had in a long time. But beneath it, there was an undercurrent of anticipation, the weight of what was coming next.

After eating, we headed to her parents' house so she could pack. Her mom and dad weren't surprised when she told them she was leaving, especially after she hadn't returned the night before. There was no shock, no protest, just a quiet understanding.

I had a feeling they had known this was inevitable, maybe even before Erica did.

Once she was ready, we loaded up her bags and made our way home.

Since we had both driven to her parents' house separately, we had to take our own cars back, leaving me alone with my thoughts for the entire drive. My emotions were tangled in a way I couldn't quite unravel—excitement, nervousness, hope. I wanted to believe this therapy session would help us, that we would walk away from it with some kind of direction, but there was a small, gnawing fear deep in my gut.

What if it didn't?

What if all of this—the space, the time apart, the reunion—had only delayed the inevitable?

When we finally pulled into the driveway, there was only an hour left before our appointment. We barely had time to breathe before rushing inside to freshen up—quick showers, fresh clothes, nerves coiling tighter with every second that passed—before we were back in the car, heading straight to the therapist's office.

Now, we're sitting in the waiting room, both of us shifting slightly in our seats, the silence between us filled with a strange kind of tension—not the bad kind, but the uncertain kind. Erica's fingers are laced tightly with mine, her grip firm, almost like she's afraid to let go.

Not that I would want her to.

The therapists redheaded assistant had greeted us when we arrived, informing us that Dr. Parker was still on her lunch break but would be with us shortly. I guess we were a little too eager to get here since we ended up arriving *fifteen minutes early*. Now, all we can do is wait.

I wonder what Erica expects from this. What does she think will help us? Does she have some idea of what she wants to hear, or is she just as lost as I am? My mind is turning over all the possibilities when the sound of a door opening pulls me from my thoughts.

A tall woman steps out, her posture composed yet welcoming. She's dressed in dark gray pants and a soft pink V-neck blouse, neatly tucked in. Her blonde hair is gathered into a sleek ponytail, not a strand out of place.

"Mr. and Mrs. Carter?" she says with a warm smile. "Please, come in and have a seat."

Erica lets out a quiet breath beside me, and we both stand. Her fingers squeeze mine one last time before she lets go, and together, we follow the therapist into her office.

I'm not sure what I expected the space to look like—something clinical, maybe. White walls, bright lights, diplomas hung up like trophies, the kind of office that feels more like a doctor's exam room than a place to talk about your deepest struggles. But this? This is different.

The room is dimly lit, but not in a cold or heavy way. Instead, it feels warm, inviting. A deep green velvet couch sits across from a wooden chair with matching upholstery, both angled in a way that makes the room feel intimate rather than staged. The walls are painted in rich, moody tones, and the lighting comes from two softly glowing lamps—one beside what I assume is Dr. Parker's chair and another next to the couch. The blinds are drawn just enough to let in streaks of natural light, casting faint golden patterns across the floor.

It's comfortable. Safe. The kind of place that doesn't scream therapy session but rather deep conversation.

I can see why people speak so highly of her.

And as I glance at Erica, watching the way her shoulders relax just a little, I realize something. Maybe, for the first time in a long time, we're in the right place.

Dr. Parker leans forward slightly, her gaze steady but kind. "So," she begins, "I understand I was recommended to you by someone?" Her tone is open, inviting, and when she looks at Erica, my wife glances at me, giving me the space to take the lead.

Clearing my throat, I answer honestly. "Yes. I was set up—well, more like tricked—into a date with someone. She told me she and her husband had come to see you. They ended up getting divorced anyway, but she said that if they had come to you sooner, there might have been more hope for them."

Dr. Parker gives a small, knowing smile and nods. "Unfortunately, not all couples who seek my help *can* be helped. When that happens, it's usually because they waited too long to admit they were unhappy. By the time they seek therapy, resentment has already taken root, and sometimes there's no way to undo that damage." She pauses briefly, then asks, "Did she tell you how I do things?" Her gaze flickers between me and Erica before settling back on me.

I shake my head. "Not really, just that you're unorthodox."

A soft laugh escapes her. "Yes, well, I hear that a lot." There's a glimmer of amusement in her brown eyes as she picks up a notebook from the small table beside her. "Let me explain how this will work."

She directs her attention to Erica, who gives a small nod, signaling she's listening.

"First, I'll start with one-on-one sessions. Brian, you'll go first. For the next five minutes, I want you to talk. Vent, rant, lay everything out. I won't interrupt or offer feedback just yet—I'll simply listen and take notes. Then we'll switch, and Erica will do the same." She flips open the notebook, pen poised, then continues.

"Once we've finished the individual sessions, all three of us will regroup here. I'll choose one word or theme from each of your sessions—something that stood out—and I'll ask you to elaborate on it. When one of you is speaking, the other will listen without interruption. After both of you have expanded on your words, you'll step out into the waiting room while I review my notes and determine the best course of action. I'll explain my reasoning, then send you home with suggestions to implement. We'll meet again in two months—sooner if necessary."

She looks between the two of us. "Any questions?"

I glance at Erica, watching as she considers the process. When she shakes her head, she looks to me expectantly, hope flickering in her blue eyes. The sight makes my chest tighten.

I force myself to look away, shifting my attention back to Dr. Parker. "None from me."

"Good. Let's get started." She stands, motioning toward the door. "Mrs. Carter, if you don't mind waiting outside, Brian and I will begin."

Erica hesitates for only a second before standing. I don't want her to leave. Something about being left alone to spill everything without her beside me feels overwhelming, but I understand that this is part of the process.

I watch as she walks to the door, my eyes following her until she disappears into the waiting room. The moment the door clicks shut, I finally exhale.

When I turn back, Dr. Parker is watching me with a small, knowing smile. "Alright, Mr. Carter," she says, adjusting the timer on her watch. "Your five minutes start now."

I wring my hands together, struggling with where to even begin. But as I stare at the floor, the words spill out before I can stop them.

"Four months ago, my wife left me."

I pause, hearing the weight of those words out loud for the first time in a long time. Two minutes ago, I wasn't sure where to start, but now I feel like baring my soul to this woman, hoping she can tell me how to put it back together again.

When Dr. Parker says nothing, simply waiting, I remember that I'm supposed to talk. So I take a deep breath and continue.

"We've been trying to conceive for about a year now. The pressure got to both of us, but I didn't realize just how much it was affecting Erica. I thought I understood, but I didn't. Not really." I let out a long breath and shake my head. "You know, a couple of months ago, right after Erica left, I went to a family gathering at my mom's. That was the first time I really understood my wife's pain."

Dr. Parker tilts her head slightly, a silent invitation to elaborate.

I run a hand through my hair and sigh. "My sister-in-law was pregnant—like, very pregnant. Erica had told me she didn't really want to go to the gathering, but I didn't get it. I didn't take the time to understand. Then, while I was inside getting a drink, I overheard my mom talking with some of the other women."

I swallow hard. The memory still burns.

"They were saying that Erica was being *selfish*. That she should be happy for my brother and his wife. That we'd get pregnant soon, and she needed to stop acting distant. But nobody knew we *were* trying. We never told anyone. We didn't want to take away from John and

Stacy's moment. And yet, there they were, judging her, not knowing how much she was hurting."

I stare at my hands, voice tight. "I held her when she cried. When people at her job got pregnant and the same damn question always came up—*'When are you going to have a baby?'* Like we weren't already doing anything we could." I shake my head. "I told her we could stop, that it wasn't worth the stress. I just wanted to take some of the pressure off of her. But instead of helping, it made things worse."

A bitter laugh escapes me, sharp and humorless.

"Looking back, I realize I've been putting pressure on her since the beginning."

Dr. Parker raises a brow slightly. I take a deep breath and explain.

"One of our earliest dates, I asked her where she saw herself in five years. I told her I saw myself married, with kids. Back then, it was just a casual conversation, but now? Now I see it differently. She knew what I wanted from the start. And here we are, six years later, still struggling to have kids. That conversation—something that was meant to be lighthearted—probably became a weight she carried every day."

I drag a hand down my face, my chest tightening. "I always wanted to be like my dad. Growing up, I thought he was the best role model. Then, after Erica and I got married, it came out that he had another family in a different town. The man who raised me, who taught me to be a good man, wasn't who I thought he was. I panicked. I started questioning everything. How could I be a good father if the man I had looked up to my whole life was capable of something like that?"

Dr. Parker remains quiet, listening.

"Eventually, Erica was the one who helped me work through it. She reminded me that his mistakes weren't mine, that I could learn from them and be better. And when I finally felt ready, we started trying."

I press my lips together, hesitating before I say the next part.

"But... what she doesn't know is that I think about it more than she realizes. More than I ever let on."

My voice drops lower, almost a whisper. "I feel like a failure sometimes. Like it's my fault she can't get pregnant. I'm terrified to go to a fertility specialist because what if I am the issue? What if she resents me?" I shake my head. "I miss when things were easy. When sex wasn't scheduled, when we didn't plan around ovulation. When I didn't feel like... like a tool, a means to an end."

Before I can say anything else, the soft chime of Dr. Parker's timer rings.

She gives me a small nod, setting her notebook aside. "That was very insightful, Brian. Thank you."

I stand as she does, heading toward the door. As I step into the waiting room, she calls for my wife.

It's her turn now.

Chapter 12

Erica

As I watch Brian step out of Dr. Parker's office, my nerves spike. For the last five minutes, I've tried to distract myself, anything to keep from wondering what he's saying. I had texted my sister, asking how her date with Greg went, and I wasn't surprised when she told me how great it had been.

Now Brian walks toward me, his expression unreadable, but the moment he reaches out and takes my hand, helping me up, warmth spreads through me. He presses a soft kiss to my forehead before letting go, and I don't think he realizes how much that small gesture steadies me, how it gives me the courage to walk into that office and face what comes next.

Dr. Parker gestures toward the couch, and I settle in, tucking my hands in my lap. She offers me a reassuring smile before picking up her notebook. "Alright, Mrs. Carter, I'm going to start the timer now.

There's no right or wrong thing to say. Just let it flow. Whenever you're ready, go ahead and begin."

She presses a button on her watch, and I take a deep breath.

"Sometimes I feel like a sorry excuse for a woman. Like I'm...*broken*."

The words fall out of my mouth before I can stop them. They hang between us, raw and vulnerable, and for a second, I want to take them back. I see a flicker of something in Dr. Parker's expression—just for a second—but she doesn't interrupt.

I exhale shakily and force myself to continue. "We've been trying to conceive for almost a year now. We finally decided that maybe it was time to see a fertility specialist. But one day, I just... panicked. I couldn't take it anymore."

Tears well up in my eyes, and I fight to blink them away, but they spill over anyway. "I am so scared that when we finally get answers, I'll be the problem. And then Brian will eventually grow to resent me." My chest tightens, the weight of those words pressing down on me. "I struggle with that fear every single day."

I reach for a tissue, dabbing at my face. My voice is softer now, but I push through. "We never told his family, or anyone, that we were trying. We wanted to, but then his brother and his wife announced their pregnancy, and we didn't want to take anything away from them. So we kept it to ourselves. And yet, every time we went to his mom's house, I'd get asked that million-dollar question—*'When will you two have one of your own?'*"

I let out a hollow laugh, shaking my head. "I get that question everywhere. At family gatherings, at work, from friends, from strangers. At first, it wasn't a big deal, but as the months went on and the tests kept coming up negative, each time felt like a small knife to my heart."

A sob breaks free, and I press a hand to my mouth, trying to steady myself. "No matter how happy I am for those around me, it sometimes feels like life is rubbing it in my face. And sometimes it's just too much. This is all I want, and yet I can't seem to have it." My voice wavers, barely above a whisper. "And nothing I say or do will fill that hole in my heart."

I close my eyes for a second, steadying my breathing, before opening them again. "I feel so alone."

The soft chime of Dr. Parker's timer rings, signaling that my five minutes are up. I lower my face into my hands, the weight of everything I just admitted crashing down on me.

A moment later, I feel a gentle touch on my shoulder. Looking up, I meet Dr. Parker's gaze, warm with understanding. "I'll give you a few moments to collect your thoughts before we continue," she says. "I need to step out for a moment."

She gives my shoulder another reassuring squeeze before leaving the room. I don't know if she actually needed to go or if she just sensed that I needed this moment alone. Either way, I'm grateful.

The quiet settles around me, but it doesn't last long. A few minutes later, I hear the door open, followed by the familiar sound of Brian's footsteps. I don't even have time to look up before I feel his arms around me, pulling me close.

No words. Just the silent comfort of his embrace.

I clutch onto him, inhaling the scent of his cologne, letting his warmth anchor me.

Dr. Parker clears her throat softly, and Brian pulls back, though he keeps one hand on my knee, his thumb stroking soothing circles against my skin.

She glances at her notebook. "I have chosen your words." Her eyes flick to Brian. "Mr. Carter, you'll go first. Erica, your job is simply to listen. Try not to interrupt or defend yourself. This isn't an attack—it's about his feelings. Just hear him out."

Brian gives a short nod, his fingers tightening slightly around mine.

"Your word, Mr. Carter, is abandoned."

My heart stops.

The word hits me like a punch to the gut. How could I have done that to him? Fresh tears spill down my cheeks before I can stop them.

Brian turns to me, his green eyes filled with an emotion I can't quite name. He lifts our joined hands to his lips, pressing a kiss to my knuckles before exhaling.

"Erica, I love you more than anything," he begins, his voice rough with emotion. "But you just... left. You didn't tell me how much you were struggling. I knew it was getting to be too much for you—I saw it. That's why I suggested we take a break from trying. But when I did, you got so upset. I wasn't trying to give up; I was trying to help. I just wanted you to be happy, and the monthly negative tests weren't helping."

His brows furrow, his grip on my hand tightening slightly. "I know things aren't easy, but I'm just as scared about the specialist as you are. I think about it more than you realize."

I open my mouth to respond, but his pleading eyes stop me. I stay silent, just as Dr. Parker instructed.

"I know on one of our first dates, we talked about where we saw ourselves in five years," he continues, his voice softer now. "I remember what I said—married, kids, the whole dream. But that was before I *knew* you. Before I realized how amazing my life is with you, no matter what happens."

I suck in a sharp breath.

"I miss when things were easy, when we could be close without it being about trying for a baby. When sex was about us, not just a schedule. After a while, I started to feel like... like a tool, just a means to an end. I felt like you only wanted me when you were ovulating. And every other day of the month? I felt invisible."

Tears spill faster now. How had I not seen this?

Brian swallows hard. "I miss you, Erica. I miss us. I don't care if we have to adopt, or use a donor, or anything else. I just want to be a parent with you. But more than that, I want my wife back."

The timer chimes softly, signaling the end of his time, but I can barely hear it over the sound of my own heartbeat pounding in my ears.

Brian lifts my hand again, pressing another lingering kiss to my fingers before letting them rest in my lap, not letting go.

Dr. Parker gives him a small nod. "Thank you, Mr. Carter." Then she turns to me.

"Mrs. Carter, your word is control."

I let out a slow, shuddering breath. I'm not surprised. Not at all.

I only need a moment before I begin.

Chapter 13

BRIAN

Erica lets out a quiet gasp at her word, and I immediately know—this is something deep, something raw. She grips my hand, her fingers curling tightly around mine, and I brace myself. Not for anger, not for blame, but for the truth she's been carrying inside her for months.

She lifts her gaze to meet mine, her blue eyes shimmering with unshed tears. "I hate not being in control right now," she admits, her voice quiet but steady. "I can control every other aspect of my life, but not this. I can't just *make* myself get pregnant. No matter how hard I try, no matter what I do... I can't."

I stay silent, just listening, absorbing every word. But she keeps searching my face, like she's afraid of what she'll find there.

With a deep breath, she continues, "Me leaving had nothing to do with how I feel about you, Brian. It had everything to do with how I feel about myself. I left because I was scared. Scared that I may never be able to give you the one thing I know you want. Scared that you'd grow to resent me for it."

Her voice cracks on the last sentence, and she quickly looks down, as if she doesn't want me to see the pain written all over her face.

God, how had I not seen the weight she was carrying alone?

She exhales shakily. "I'm sorry you were hurt when I left. I really am. But if I had told you I needed space, you would have talked me out of it. And I couldn't let that happen. Because in those four months, without the pressure, without the scheduled trying, without constantly feeling like I was failing you, I found myself again. I remembered that I am more than just a woman struggling to get pregnant."

She looks back up at me, and the pain in her eyes nearly shatters me.

I reach up and wipe away the single tear that escapes, and she leans into my touch.

"I know you don't forgive me," she whispers, "but I hope you understand now."

I do. God, I do.

She takes a trembling breath. "Every time someone around me got pregnant, I couldn't help but wonder—what's wrong with me? Why not us? Don't we deserve that, too? I started avoiding certain places, even taking different routes home so I wouldn't have to pass the park. Seeing all those parents with their kids... it broke me a little more every time. I am always happy for the people in my life who are blessed with children, but it feels like a dream slipping further and further away from us."

A sob racks through her, and it takes everything in me not to pull her into my arms right now.

I hadn't known. I hadn't realized just how much this was breaking her, how much of it she carried in silence.

And suddenly, I think back to all the little arguments over driving routes, over the smallest things, the ones I dismissed as meaningless. She always wanted to take a different way. Maybe she was just looking for a new path, some road that didn't constantly remind her of what we didn't have. I never stopped to ask why.

I should have asked why.

Erica sniffles, composing herself slightly. "Now that I've had that time, I get it. I understand my emotions better. And I feel like I'm finally in the right mindset to take the next steps. I'm ready to surrender my control to the doctors and get answers. No matter what they say."

She pauses, then chokes out, "I just need you to understand that I can't control this, Brian."

Her voice is so raw, so desperate, that my chest physically aches.

Tears spill freely down her cheeks now, and when the soft chime of the timer rings, I barely hear it. I am drowning in the pain swirling in my wife's eyes.

Dr. Parker leans back in her chair, watching us carefully. "That was very insightful, Mrs. Carter." She closes her notebook. "I'm going to step out for a few moments to review my notes and come up with a plan for the two of you. I'll give you some time to collect your thoughts before we continue."

She stands and moves toward the door, but before she can pass me, I clear my throat. "Thank you."

She pauses, offering me a small nod before slipping out of the office, leaving us alone.

And the moment the door shuts, I don't even hesitate. I pull Erica into my arms, wrapping her up tightly against my chest.

She doesn't just cry—she breaks.

I rub slow, soothing circles on her back, letting her sob into my shirt, letting her release everything she's been holding in. There's nothing I can say to take away her pain, nothing that will erase the months she's spent feeling alone in this.

So, I don't try to fix it.

I just hold her.

We stay wrapped in each other's arms for a long moment, her body slowly relaxing against mine as her breathing evens out. When she finally pulls away, her eyes are red-rimmed but calmer. I cup her cheek, brushing my thumb over her soft skin before pressing a lingering kiss to her lips. When I pull back, I search her face, wanting her to hear me—really hear me.

"I don't blame you for anything, baby," I tell her, my voice low but firm. "We're going to get through this together. We'll figure it out, and we'll get back to where we were. But most importantly, you need to be okay. I need *you*. Please don't shut me out again. Let me help. Don't leave... don't go through this alone."

Her lips part, as if she wants to respond, but before she can, the door opens, and Dr. Parker steps back into the room. Erica's fingers tighten around mine in a reassuring squeeze before we both turn our attention to her.

Dr. Parker settles into her chair, her expression warm but professional. "First, I want to thank you both for trusting me with this. I know it wasn't easy to open up, especially about something so painful. But the fact that you were able to do so—together—tells me that you're both willing to put in the work to rebuild your marriage." She pauses, flipping open her notes.

I take the moment to glance at Erica, only to find her already looking at me. There's something softer in her gaze, a small smile playing on her lips. I return it with one of my own before we both refocus on Dr. Parker.

"Second," she continues, "I have a few recommendations that I believe will help. One of them is a little unconventional, but I ask that you keep an open mind."

Erica and I exchange a look before nodding, signaling for her to continue.

"I'd like you both to take two quizzes—one to determine your love languages and another to explore your sexual preferences, a kink test."

I raise an eyebrow, skeptical. A kink test? I don't see how that's relevant to fixing our problems.

Apparently, Erica is thinking the same thing. "I don't understand," she says. "Sex has been one of our biggest struggles because of the pressure we both feel. How is a kink test supposed to help with that?"

Dr. Parker smiles knowingly. "You're right—the issue isn't sex itself. The issue is the pressure surrounding it, the expectations, the obligation. Over time, that pressure has stripped away the intimacy and fun that should naturally be a part of your physical relationship. Taking the test will help you rediscover what excites you, what makes sex something to look forward to again. It's not about adding pressure—it's about taking it away and bringing curiosity and playfulness back into your connection."

That makes a lot more sense.

She shifts slightly, crossing her legs and placing her notebook in her lap. "Now, to help rekindle the emotional spark, I also want you to take the love languages test. Once you know each other's love languages, start making small, thoughtful gestures that align with them."

She turns to me first. "For example, if Erica's love language is acts of service, do something around the house that she'd normally do herself. Pick up her favorite food and surprise her at work. If it's quality time, plan an at-home date night. There are plenty of ideas online. If it's gift-giving, pick up something small—a book, a trinket, a thrift store find—just to show you were thinking of her. If it's physical touch, be intentional about small touches throughout the day. Sit closer on the couch, play with her hair, give her a massage. And if it's words of affirmation, make sure you're expressing how much you appreciate her. Tell her when she looks beautiful, when you're grateful for something she's done, or just remind her why you love her."

I find myself nodding along. It sounds... simple. Manageable.

Dr. Parker continues, "The key here is attentiveness. When your partner suddenly starts receiving love in the way they understand it best, it creates a deeper sense of connection. And as you rebuild that foundation, the physical part of your relationship will naturally begin to heal as well."

Erica exhales softly, looking thoughtful. "When you put it that way, it actually makes a lot of sense."

I glance at her and find her eyes filled with hope.

"For now," Dr. Parker says, "I suggest focusing on love languages for the rest of the week. No pressure for sex—just rebuild anticipation and intimacy. However, that doesn't mean avoiding all physical touch. You can still enjoy foreplay, oral sex, mutual masturbation—anything that feels good without the expectation of intercourse. The idea is to shift away from obligation and back toward desire."

That makes sense too. I already feel lighter at the thought of not treating sex like a job.

"I also suggest taking both quizzes today and discussing the results," she adds. "Try out some of the lower-risk things on your kink test and see what feels right. Then, plan a date for the weekend—something fun, something just for the two of you. Let it build naturally toward sex, rather than scheduling it like a chore."

I glance at Erica again, watching her reaction. Her lips press together as she considers it all, and then she nods. "I like that plan."

"Me too," I agree.

Dr. Parker closes her notebook. "Great. Do either of you have any questions?"

"No, I think it's pretty straightforward," Erica answers, before looking to me.

"None here."

She stands, and we follow. "While I stepped out earlier, I checked my schedule. I have an opening for a follow-up in two months, on the tenth. Does an evening appointment work for you both?"

I pull out my phone, checking our calendar. "Yeah, that date is open. Can we do five-thirty?"

Her assistant, a redhead sitting at the front desk, turns the computer screen to check. "Dr. Parker has a session until five-forty-five, but she's available at six."

I nod, adjusting the time in my phone. "Six works."

"Perfect," she says, handing us a small card with two website links. "These are the quizzes I'd like you to use. If at any point you feel like my recommendations aren't working, reach out. Otherwise, I'll see you both in two months."

Erica and I exchange one last glance before turning toward the door. As we step out into the cool evening air, she lets out a deep breath, as if releasing months of tension. I reach for her hand, interlacing our fingers, and she squeezes back.

For the first time in a long time, I feel like we're on the right path.

Like maybe—just maybe—we can find our way back to each other.

Chapter 14

Erica

My mind is racing. The love languages made sense, but the *kink* test? That's something I can't quite wrap my head around. We've been together for over five years, so I think we know what we like. But if Dr. Parker thinks it will help, I'm willing to try anything.

"How about you take the tests on the way home?" Brian suggests as we walk up to the car. "Then, when we get there, you can take a bath to relax while I finish. Afterward, we can order dinner and talk everything over. I think we both need time to process this."

"That sounds like a plan," I agree, standing on my toes to kiss him on the cheek. He opens the car door for me, and I hold my phone in one hand, the paper with the website addresses in the other.

I must have been staring at them because, when Brian gets in the car, he takes my phone and the paper, typing in one of the sites. "Start with the love languages one, then go with the other," he says, handing the phone back to me.

With a grateful smile, I start the quiz. When I'm finished, I'm not surprised by the results. I know I appreciate acts of service and quality time over the others. I feel like the luckiest girl in the world when Brian does things for me so I don't have to, or when we do things together, like going to a new restaurant followed by drinks at our favorite bar—though it's been a while since we've done that.

I look out the window to gather my thoughts. How did we let things get this bad? I know it's not all on me, but I pulled away. I left. Brian was there, trying to get me to talk, but I couldn't see it. I was so caught up in my own feelings, never considering his.

Tears slip down my face as I watch the world blur by. I should finish the other quiz, but my head is too full to focus. So I sit quietly, lost in the "could've" and "should've" racing through my thoughts.

Brian squeezes my hand gently, pulling me back into the present. "We're almost home," he says. "Why don't you start the other quiz now? I know that look—you're getting lost in your head again."

With a small nod, I agree, more to him than the quiz. I still can't quite bring myself to process everything that was said back in Dr. Parker's office. With the other quiz open, I choose the in-depth option and begin answering the questions.

By the time we pull up to the house, I'm three-quarters through. "How's it going over there?" Brian asks.

"I still have to finish. I'm about three-quarters of the way done. It's pretty in-depth, though. Some of the questions have caught my attention," I explain. "Instead of a yes-or-no or multiple-choice format, there's a seven-point scale ranging from strongly disagree to strongly agree. For example, if I'm unsure but open to trying something, I can choose an option between neutral and strongly agree. I think this makes the results more accurate."

Brian nods. "Sounds interesting. Anyway, what are you thinking for dinner? I'll place the order while you get cleaned up, then we can talk about the results."

"Pizza sounds really good," I smile. I don't even need to say where from—he already knows it's Hawaiian with pepperoni instead of ham and jalapeños. My stomach growls just thinking about it.

"Go ahead, I'll place the order," he says, laughing. I lean over and give him a quick kiss before heading inside to finish the quiz.

I start the bath, then sit at the vanity to finish. My highest result surprises me, but also makes sense. I like when things are done my way. But there are other things that intrigue me too—things I hadn't considered before. Some of them are even a little outside my comfort zone, like being watched or watching.

With these thoughts in my head, I move to the bathroom, strip off my clothes, and sink into the warm bath water. The heat eases my muscles, and the tension from the day begins to slip away. For the first time in what feels like forever, I can fully relax. I let my eyes fall shut and focus on my breathing. It feels good just to be for a moment, to let everything else melt away.

I must've drifted off, because the sound of knocking startles me awake. The water is cool now, the scent of lavender and vanilla almost gone. He cracks the door and pokes his head in.

"The food just arrived," Brian says, eyes taking me in. "I'll open a bottle of wine and meet you downstairs." He winks before closing the door behind him.

"Okay, I'll be down in a few." I say, pulling the plug and stepping out of the tub, wrapping a towel around myself.

When I enter the bedroom, I slip on some panties and a tank top. I walk over to the closet, but something catches my eye. On the edge of my side of the bed, draped haphazardly, is the nightgown I was looking for. When I pick it up and prepare to put it on, I notice a stain. Immediately, I know what it is. I've seen it on the sheets before.

I decide to put on shorts instead and head downstairs to dinner, where I'll bring up my little discovery.

The smell of pizza hits my nose as I make my way into the dining room. My stomach growls loudly, and I smile when I see Brian has already opened the box and placed the two wine glasses on the table. No plates. Of course. I love when we eat this way.

"I'm so hungry," I say as I sit across from him. I grab a slice and take a big bite. A small satisfied moan escapes me. This pizza never gets old.

We eat in silence for a while before Brian breaks it. "So, I was really surprised by my results." He looks almost embarrassed, which only makes me more intrigued.

"Is that so?" I ask, smiling. "I was surprised by a couple of my results too, but for the most part, I think it hit the nail on the head."

He clears his throat. "I mean, my results made sense, but also threw me for a loop." He glances down at his pizza awkwardly. It's so endearing to see him like this.

"Bri, you know I won't judge you for anything, right? Your results won't make me think any less of you," I reassure him, reaching across the table to hold his hand. His shoulders relax, and he breathes deeply.

Here it comes...

Chapter 15

Brian

A strange nervous energy settles deep in my gut, tightening with every passing second. I know Erica won't judge me, not really, but admitting something that contradicts everything I was raised to believe? That's something else entirely. Men are supposed to be dominant. Strong. In control. But now, faced with the truth of my test results, I feel anything *but* in control.

Erica squeezes my hand gently, reassuringly, but I still find it difficult to lift my eyes to hers. Clearing my throat, I force the words out in a rush before I can change my mind. "I'm a submissive."

The silence that follows is unbearable. I finally glance up, searching her face, but I can't quite read her expression. Her blue eyes are locked onto mine, reflecting something—heat? Embarrassment? I can't tell. Her posture is tense, her shoulders slightly stiff, but she doesn't let go of my hand.

Seconds stretch into eternity. *Say something, baby, please.* I feel my stomach drop further into my gut. I go to pull my hand back, but the moment I do, she suddenly snaps out of her thoughts.

"Why are you nervous?" Her voice is soft, genuinely confused.

I let out a heavy sigh, feeling the weight of my tension in every breath. "Because I should be more dominant," I admit. My shoulders sag as the words leave my lips, as if voicing the thought makes it even more real.

Her eyes widen in shock, and I hurry to clarify, "Granted, switch was on my list too, but like fourth or fifth. Submissive was at the top." I drop my gaze, feeling exposed in a way I never have before. The insecurity gnaws at me, making me question everything.

But then—soft laughter.

I snap my head up, eyebrows furrowing as I watch Erica struggle to hold back her amusement. A sting of hurt spreads through me, quickly shifting to frustration.

"It's really not funny," I mutter, going to pull my hand from hers again. This time, she lets me go.

Her laughter fades instantly, replaced by something softer. "Bri, I wasn't laughing at you. I swear. It's just—" she shakes her head, biting her lip as if trying to contain another smile, "—my top result was switch. Which means I apparently like dominating too."

I blink at her. "You're joking."

She grins. "Nope."

For a moment, we just stare at each other, processing. Then, slowly, she stands from her seat and moves around the table. I watch as she steps between my legs, then waves a hand, signaling for me to scoot my chair back.

I oblige without hesitation.

The second I do, she swings one leg over mine, settling herself onto my lap. My hands find her hips instinctively, gripping the curve of her waist as she drapes her arms around my neck.

"I really do love how it feels when I'm the one telling you what to do," she murmurs, her voice laced with teasing warmth.

Before I can respond, she leans in, pressing her lips to mine. The kiss is soft at first, slow and deliberate, but it quickly shifts into something deeper. Something heated. She runs her tongue along my bottom lip, seeking permission, and I part for her easily.

At first, we fight for dominance, both pushing, both taking. But then—*fuck*—she runs her nails along my scalp, gripping my hair, tugging just enough to send a shiver down my spine. My body reacts before my mind catches up. I let go. I follow her lead.

The moment I do, a low moan slips from her throat.

She pulls back slightly, breathless. "I think if we gave it a shot, you'd enjoy it," she whispers.

I stare at her, my head still swimming in the sensations of her touch. It's hard for me to picture myself in that role—completely at the mercy of a woman, of *her*, in an intimate setting.

"I don't know, baby," I say, exhaling heavily. "I just... I don't know how I feel about it." I run a hand through my hair, staring at the floor. "This is the last thing I expected. And with the way I was raised, it goes against everything my father drilled into me about what it means to be a man." I meet her eyes, my throat tightening. "So right now? I don't feel like one."

She watches me, her gaze filled with nothing but understanding. No judgment. No frustration. Just patience.

"I know it's messed up," I admit, shaking my head. "But I'll try. I just need a little time to wrap my head around it."

A soft smile plays on her lips as she nods. "Of course. I understand." She reaches for my hand, squeezing gently. "I want to help you through this. Maybe if I give you an idea of something I'd like, it might help you?"

I hesitate, considering her words. There's no harm in just talking about it. No pressure. No expectations. Just exploring the idea. Finally, I nod.

Her face lights up, her excitement so contagious my chest tightens with something warm, something deeper than just desire. God, I'd do anything to make her happy.

She shifts in my lap, wiggling her hips slightly as she settles in, and then—she smirks.

"So, one of my results was rigger," she purrs, watching my reaction carefully. "I want to know how you'd feel if I tied you to the bed and made you lick my pussy."

I swallow hard. That actually sounds really sexy. *Too* sexy.

Noticing my reaction, she grinds down on me, teasing. "And what if I made you wear a cock ring while I sucked you off? All while you made me come with that talented tongue of yours?"

Fuck. My fingers tighten on her hips as my cock stirs beneath her.

She leans in, dragging her tongue up the column of my throat, and whispers, "And what if I rode you like a toy, taking exactly what I want, before I untied you... and took the cock ring off so you could bend me over my vanity?" She nips at my ear. "I've always loved the way you look when you come so hard you can barely stand."

Jesus Christ. That doesn't sound bad at all.

The idea of her using my body to get herself off while I'm helpless to do anything but watch the sheer ecstasy on her face? I'm so fucking hard it aches.

"Fuck, baby," I growl, grabbing her wrist and guiding her hand down my chest, over my throbbing cock. "I think you already know I'd like that."

Her wicked smile sends a shiver down my spine as she unzips my jeans and drops to her knees. With one swift motion, she takes me into her mouth, her tongue swirling lazily around the tip. A deep groan rumbles through me, but I don't want teasing touches. I want more.

Gripping the back of her neck, I try to thrust up, but she presses my hips back down, taking control. This time, she moves faster, taking me deeper. My jaw clenches. It takes everything in me not to fuck that pretty mouth of hers.

"Shit," I grit out, my breathing ragged. "Erica, baby, if you don't slow down, I'm going to—"

She stops suddenly, leaving me painfully hard, and stands. My head is spinning, but she just smirks and moves the pizza box aside before leaning back on the table.

"I want to watch you stroke your cock while I touch myself," she says, her voice husky.

Heat rushes through me at the sheer filth of her words. Before I do as she asks, I hook my fingers into her shorts and slide them down her legs. She raises a brow but doesn't stop me.

As soon as she's bare, she spreads her legs wider, knowing exactly why I did it.

"Is this better?" she teases.

I wrap my hand around my cock, stroking slowly, eyes locked on her. "Much."

She trails her fingers over her breasts, teasing her nipples through the thin, pale-purple fabric of her tank top. My breathing grows heavier as she drags her other hand lower, parting herself for me.

She circles her clit with a delicate touch, a slow, low moan slipping from her lips. She leans up slightly, eyes locked on me. "Yes... work that dick for me."

I stroke faster, matching her movements, hypnotized by the way she touches herself. The sounds she makes drive me insane, pushing me closer, harder, faster.

"Fuck, love, I'm so close," I groan, my body taut, on the verge of breaking.

She suddenly tenses, her voice sharp. "Don't you fucking dare come until I do."

The pure command in her tone sends a shiver down my spine. My entire body reacts—I stop instantly, holding back. I watch her, breathing hard, as my fingers itch to touch her.

"Do you want to make me come?" she asks, her voice softer now, coaxing.

I nod.

"Then go ahead," she whispers, spreading her legs wider. "Make me come."

I don't hesitate.

Leaning forward, I run my tongue over her already-swollen clit, savoring the way she gasps. Slipping a finger inside her, I press deep, adding a second as I curl them just right, thrusting in sync with my tongue.

"Yes, right there," she moans. "Stroke your cock while you fuck me with your fingers."

Obeying, I take myself in hand again, matching the rhythm. The way she moves beneath me, the way she tightens around my fingers, the way she gasps—it's all too much.

She's close, teetering on the edge, moaning uncontrollably, her body trembling. And when I know she's seconds from unraveling, I pull back, leaving her breathless.

Erica sits up, watching me, a flicker of hesitation crossing her features. Then, straightening her back, she meets my eyes with purpose.

"Tell me where you want to come," she commands.

I don't even think. The words tumble out, raw and desperate. "Your pussy. I want to come on your pussy."

A slow, wicked smile spreads across her face. She doesn't lay back—she stays up, watching, making sure she sees every second of my release. It only takes a few more strokes before the pleasure surges through me, my spine arching, my cock pulsing as I spill onto her.

And all she does is look up at me, completely in control.

I lean in, capturing her lips in a deep kiss, still breathless, still buzzing.

"Good boy," she whispers against my lips.

I freeze.

A jolt of heat rushes through me, and I realize—I liked that. More than I expected. My cock twitches, already hardening again.

Before I can say a word, she backpedals. "I'm sorry, I just thought—"

I cut her off with another kiss, deeper this time, my hands tangling in her hair.

"I like it," I admit, my voice rough. "I started getting hard again." I take a breath, staring into her dark, expectant eyes. "And to answer your question—I do think I can do this."

A slow smile spreads across her lips as happiness glitters in her eyes.

"If it's okay with you," I murmur, brushing a thumb over her cheek, "I have an idea that might help us both."

She nods eagerly, excitement dancing across her face.

If only she knew what I was about to suggest.

Chapter 16

Erica

I don't know what came over me when I called him a good boy—but the way he reacted? The way his body responded? *That* excited me. More than I expected.

And it wasn't just that. Being in control like that, knowing I dictated his pleasure, felt intoxicating. It was empowering in a way I hadn't experienced before. Seeing him so turned on, so desperate for me, filled me with confidence. It made me feel sexy. Wanted.

Desired.

And I haven't felt that in a long time.

Brian clears his throat, shifting beside me. "So... about my idea," he says hesitantly, rubbing the back of his neck. "I think it could help us both figure things out. I'm not sure how you'll feel about it, but it's just a suggestion. If you have a better one, I'm all ears."

I tilt my head, intrigued. "I'm open to just about anything," I say, offering him an encouraging smile.

His lips twitch at that. "How would you feel about watching some porn with me?" He hesitates, then adds, "I think it could give me a better sense of what I might—or might not—like."

I blink. Well, that wasn't what I expected.

I hesitate. "I don't know, Bri. You know I don't really care for it, but I also don't mind if you do." A million thoughts run through my mind, yet I can't seem to settle on a single one.

"I know you don't," he says softly. "But the thing is... I liked what we did. A lot." His cheeks flush slightly, but he holds my gaze. "I just—I need to understand my boundaries. My limits. What turns me on and what doesn't." He sighs. "The idea of being submissive is still new to me, and honestly? I think watching other men in that role might help me be more comfortable with it."

That actually makes sense.

I nod slowly. "If you think it'll help, then go for it." I hesitate, feeling unexpectedly shy. "I, um... I was thinking about looking online too."

Brian's brows furrow. "For what?"

I bite my lip, my face heating. "Toys."

His lips curl into a slow smirk. "Am I not enough for you?" His voice is teasing, but the second he finishes the sentence, he snickers—and so do I.

"Oh my god, shut up," I laugh, nudging him playfully.

He chuckles. "I couldn't resist." He shakes his head. "That's actually a great idea. Do you want to look together, or would you rather do it alone?"

I consider it. "Together."

"Good," he says, grinning. "I'd like that."

After putting away the pizza and tidying up the kitchen, we head upstairs.

As I step into the bedroom, something catches my eye. My nightgown. It's draped over the bed, and Brian is standing beside it, holding the fabric between his fingers.

I pause in the doorway, leaning against the frame. "I was wondering what happened to that."

His head snaps toward me, eyes wide. "I, uh…" He clears his throat, shifting awkwardly. He looks so cute when he's flustered.

"Bri, I'm not mad," I reassure him, crossing the room. "But I would like to know what happened."

He exhales, rubbing a hand over his face. "While you were gone…" He hesitates, then sighs. "I got turned on. And I, uh, took care of it." He winces slightly. "But it wasn't enough. I wasn't satisfied. I couldn't even sleep in here. So I crashed in the other room instead."

I nod slowly, absorbing his words. But what sticks out the most is what he says next.

"Yesterday, I was just—frustrated. Unsatisfied. Tired of feeling that way. So when I woke up aching for you, and you still weren't here, and we still weren't okay…" He trails off, swallowing thickly. "I just… I needed something."

I feel that. Because he's right. We weren't okay. And that's on me. I left.

I ran.

"And?" I press gently.

His grip tightens slightly on the fabric. "And so I came in here, grabbed your nightgown, and laid it out on the bed." His voice drops, his eyes flicking to mine. "Then I took some lotion, and I—" He pauses, shifting his weight. "I made myself come all over it."

A sudden heat floods my belly.

His voice lowers further. "And the thought of making you wear it afterward? Of fucking you in it?" His throat bobs as he swallows. "It got me off—so hard. And for the first time in days, I felt satisfied."

Oh.

Oh.

That's why he was nervous.

I step closer, heart hammering. "I won't lie," I murmur, pressing my palm against his chest. "That's actually... really hot."

His breath catches. "You think so?"

I nod, my fingers trailing up to his jaw. "Maybe we could act it out sometime."

His pulse spikes beneath my touch.

"You'd do that?" His voice is hoarse, his green eyes darkening with something primal.

I smirk. "Of course. Just so you know—hearing you describe it? Kinda turned me on."

His restraint snaps. He pulls me into a kiss—deep, slow, reverent. Like he's making up for lost time.

I smile against his lips before pulling away slightly, resting my forehead against his. "I missed you."

His arms tighten around me, and he guides me onto the bed, settling us so my head is resting on his chest, his arm draped securely around my waist.

"Bri..." My voice is quieter now. "I'm so sorry I just left. I didn't think you'd understand. But now I realize... how could you? I never talked to you about it. And when you tried to help—when you suggested a break—I got mad at you." My throat tightens, tears stinging my eyes.

He presses a kiss to my hair. "It's okay, baby. We'll get past this."

I nod against his chest, exhaling slowly.

After a moment, he reaches for his phone, and we start looking through different websites. It takes a few tries to find one we both like, but eventually, we do.

Scrolling through the couples section, we come across some remote-controlled toys, which seem fun, but then another idea strikes me.

"What if we got something I could use to tease you too?" I glance up at him.

He looks down at me, considering. "Depends on what it is... but yeah, I think I'd be open to that."

Noted.

As we continue browsing, we come across the strap-on section. Neither of us says anything, but Brian doesn't immediately scroll past it either.

Interesting.

I tuck that thought away for later.

But then, another idea invades my mind—one I can't seem to shake. One I don't want to shake.

And suddenly, I know exactly what I want to suggest next.

Chapter 17

BRIAN

After spending the night talking about our love language results, we fell asleep wrapped around each other. It was the best sleep I've had in *months*. For the first time in a long time, I feel like we were on the same page—like we were going to be okay.

With Erica still asleep beside me, I decide to put the doctor's advice to the test. Actions over words. Show her, don't just tell her. I carefully slip out of bed, throw on some sweatpants and a gray shirt, then pad downstairs to make her coffee.

But the moment I open the fridge, I realize a flaw in my plan. The only coffee creamer we have expired two months ago. Not surprising, considering I take mine black, but disappointing nonetheless.

With a new plan forming, I grab my keys and head out to the nearest coffee shop—her favorite one. By the time I walk out with her go-to order, a blended caramel macchiato with vanilla and extra caramel drizzle, along with a chocolate croissant and a strawberry Danish, I'm feeling pretty good about myself. Then, as I pass a flower shop, I make another quick stop. Daisies. Simple, but they remind me of her—bright and beautiful.

On the drive home, I make one more call. A surprise I know she'll love.

When I step through the door, I expect to find her still curled up in bed, but instead, I find her in the kitchen, standing in front of the open refrigerator, peering inside. She's wearing light yellow silk shorts, the kind with delicate black lace around the hem. They're just short enough that the curve of her ass peeks out when she shifts her weight. Her matching camisole had ridden up slightly, exposing the band of her dark purple panties. Her hair is in a messy bun, and she's barefoot.

Then, as if the universe is testing me, she bends over to search the lower shelf.

I barely hold back a groan.

Setting the coffee, pastries, and flowers on the counter, I step up behind her, placing my hands on her hips and pulling her back against me. She gasps and nearly jumps.

"If I'd known you looked like this when I woke up, I wouldn't have left," I murmur into her ear.

She lets out a small laugh. "I wondered where you were."

"What are you looking for?"

She sighs dramatically. "Something with caffeine. You know I don't like my coffee black, and apparently, that creamer has expired." She gestures toward the bottle on the counter with mock betrayal.

"Well, good thing I know my wife." I reach past her, grabbing the coffee and pastries. As soon as I hand them to her, her eyes light up, and the smile that spreads across her face makes my chest tighten in the best way.

"You got me coffee?" She sounds almost surprised.

"Of course. I was going to make you some, but when I saw the creamer situation, I figured I'd do one better." I nod toward the flowers. "Picked these up, too."

The joy in her eyes turns glossy with unshed tears, and suddenly, I feel like the biggest idiot for ever letting myself stop doing these things for her. It took less than an hour out of my day, and now, she'll carry this happiness with her.

"You got me flowers?" Her voice wavers slightly.

I shrug. "Walked past the shop and thought of you."

She sets her coffee down and wraps her arms around my torso, pressing herself against me. I hold her tightly, just breathing her in, grounding myself in the moment.

We stay like that until my phone rings.

I sigh heavily. Erica doesn't need to ask who it was—she recognizes the ringtone. My mother.

Declining the call, I look up to find her watching me, eyebrows raised.

"What?" I ask.

She tilts her head. "I've never seen you ignore a call from your mom like that. I mean, you've let them go to voicemail before, but never with that kind of... finality." She studies me for a second. "What aren't you telling me?"

"Nothing," I say too quickly.

"Brian." Her tone leaves no room for argument.

I exhale sharply. "Fine. I'll tell you everything. Let me at least make a cup of coffee first."

She nods, so I go through the motions, buying myself a few extra moments before I sit down and lay it all out. Every last thing my mother said. Every hurtful comment. Every assumption.

When I finish, I expect Erica to be upset—maybe even angry—but she just sits there, her expression unreadable.

"You're not surprised," I realize. "Has she said things like this to you before?"

She sighs, taking my hand. "Brian, that's just how people are. They don't know the full story, so they assume." She squeezes my fingers. "But you can't cut your mom out for something she said when she didn't know the truth. Do you really think she would've said those things if she'd known?"

I clench my jaw. "It doesn't matter. She still said them. It hurt you to be around people when we were trying so hard, and it just wasn't happening."

Erica's eyes soften. "Brian, it didn't hurt seeing other people happy. I was happy for them. What hurt was that it wasn't us."

Something about the way she said that hit me like a gut punch. Of course. My wife would never resent someone else's happiness—she'd just wonder why we couldn't have the same.

"I get it now," I admit.

She nods. "I think you should talk to her."

I run a hand through my hair. "I don't get how you're so unbothered by all this."

"I'm not unbothered." She sighs. "It sucks that she doesn't know me well enough to realize I'd never think that way. But I have to give her grace. She didn't know we were trying. If I were in her shoes, I don't know that I wouldn't have said the same things." She meets my gaze. "But now she knows the truth. The least we can do is talk to her."

I stare at her, letting her words sink in. She's right.

With a deep sigh, I nod. "Fine. But not yet. My focus is on us and the family we want to build."

She smiles, and I pull her in for a kiss.

"Oh, and I have one more surprise for you," I murmur. "While I was out, I called Mandy. She had a last-minute cancellation and said she could squeeze you in at the spa in two hours."

Her face lights up, and for the second time that morning, I'm reminded just how much these little things mean to her.

"Are you serious?" she beams.

"Yep. So you better get moving if you want to make it."

Laughing, she kisses me quickly before rushing upstairs to get ready.

While she's upstairs, I tidy up the living room before starting a quick breakfast, nothing fancy, just a couple slices of toast with bacon. Something she can eat on the road—just small mundane tasks to try not to think. But no matter what I do, my mind keeps circling back to last night.

To the things we talked about. To the things I'm still thinking about.

After about twenty minutes, Erica comes downstairs wearing black joggers and a light purple cropped hoodie, paired with her usual slip-on sneakers. Her blonde hair is pulled into a loose ponytail, and she's completely bare-faced—no makeup, no effort. And yet, she's still effortlessly beautiful.

She walks over to the fridge, grabbing a bottle of water, and my eyes can't help but drift lower. The way those joggers hug her curves... yeah, I'm definitely staring.

She turns around just as I glance up, catching me in the act. There's a knowing smirk on her lips, and I roll my eyes with a grin.

"What? You look hot like that," I say with a casual shrug.

She laughs, shaking her head. "Well, I'm heading out. I want to stop and get Mandy a boba tea on the way, and I need to fill up my car too. I'll call you when I'm on my way home."

She presses a quick kiss to my lips and takes the food I offer before heading out the door, leaving me alone with my thoughts.

At first, I keep busy. I throw in some laundry, making a point not to wash her nightgown, then unpack both of our bags and put everything away. But I know this is just mindless work, an attempt to distract myself from what I really want to think about.

And now, I can't avoid it any longer.

Sinking onto our dark green couch, I pull out my phone. Erica's comfortable with me watching porn, so I don't hesitate as I open a site. The search bar at the top tempts me, and before I can overthink it, I type in the word that has been haunting my thoughts.

Pegging.

Even as I stare at the search results, shame knots in my stomach. I shouldn't want this. But something deep inside me won't let it go.

I don't let myself scroll—I know if I do, I'll back out. Instead, I click on the first video that comes up.

I don't know what I was expecting. Maybe a man bound and helpless. But *this*? This is something else entirely.

The woman sits on the edge of the couch, her legs spread, and the man is between them, devouring her with desperate hunger. Her head is thrown back, her fingers tangled in his hair, keeping him exactly where she wants him. She's guiding him, controlling him. I can't hear them—I've kept the volume off—but I don't need to. The scene in front of me says enough.

Her body tightens, trembling, and still, he doesn't let up. She wraps her legs around him, pulling him up her body, and when their lips meet, she licks along his mouth, tasting herself on his lips. Then, she bites his lower lip, tugging it before slipping her tongue into his mouth, sucking him in.

I watch, mesmerized, as she slides her hands down his body until she grips his cock. His entire body jerks at her touch. With one hand, she guides him to her entrance, and with the other, she snakes around his waist, pulling his hips toward her.

She doesn't just let him take control. No—her hands grip his hips, setting the rhythm herself. Pushing him back, pulling him forward. Again and again. Harder. Deeper. He tries to keep up, to match the pace she's setting, but she's in charge here.

She says something to him, and his hand moves to her throat, the other gripping her wrists. A flicker of something dangerous and exciting sparks between them. She speaks again, and I see him hesitate—just for a second—before trying to recover, finding the rhythm she demands. But she only shakes her head. *No.*

For the first time, I'm tempted to turn the sound on, to hear what they're saying. But I resist.

Then, the scene shifts.

She stands, stepping out of view, while he sits back on the couch, stroking himself. I fast-forward until she returns—only now, she's wearing a harness. The camera moves to the side, revealing a blue silicone dildo strapped to her hips.

The man doesn't look ashamed. He doesn't look nervous or uncertain. If anything, he looks... excited.

She picks up a bottle of lube from the floor, squeezing some onto the toy. And then—she waits.

At first, I don't understand why. But then, he reaches out, wrapping his fingers around it, stroking it with slow, deliberate movements. He's the one coating it in lube, preparing it.

When he's ready, she presses him back by his shoulders, lifting his legs over hers as she kneels between his thighs. Another stream of lube spills onto him before she lines the toy up with his entrance. She moves carefully at first, easing it in, letting him adjust.

But he doesn't look uncomfortable. He doesn't look like he's in pain. If anything, he looks like he's trying not to come.

She starts slow, her movements controlled, measured. Then, little by little, she moves faster, harder.

The man drops his head to the side, murmuring something, and curiosity gets the best of me. I turn up the volume.

"This is what you get when you don't listen," she says, her voice low and breathless. "This is how I expect you to fuck me."

That's when I notice two things.

One—she's moving exactly as she had guided him before, teaching him through action.

And two—I'm painfully, unbearably turned on.

"Yes, ma'am," he breathes.

"Good boy," she purrs. "Why don't you play with that hard cock of yours while I fuck your ass?"

He moans in response, wrapping his hand around himself, and when she spits on his cock, I realize—she's not punishing him. She's giving him what he needs. What he craves.

"Oh, fuck, yes—I'm close. Please let me come. I'll listen next time, I promise," he groans, rocking his hips, desperate for more.

She pauses. "Tell me what you want."

"Hard. Harder. I need you to fuck my ass harder. Please."

She freezes, waiting.

"Ma'am—please, ma'am!" he begs, seeming to correct his error. And then she thrusts into him, hard, and his eyes roll back. "Thank you, ma'am," he gasps.

"That's more like it," she murmurs. "Be a good boy and come for me. Come all over your stomach."

Her movements turn relentless, pounding into him as he strokes himself furiously. It doesn't take long—less than a minute before he's coming, his release splattering across his chest as his whole body trembles.

"Thank you, thank you, thank you," he chants as she pulls out.

The video ends. Another starts loading.

But I don't press play.

Instead, I close the site, pushing my pants down just enough to free my aching cock. The thought of Erica doing that to me is too much, and I don't last long at all.

When I finally come down from it, my breath still heavy, I pull my phone back up—not to watch another video.

But to place an order.

For everything we'll need to make this new fantasy a reality.

Chapter 18

Erica

The spa was exactly what I needed. The warmth of the sauna, the scent of lavender in the air, the skilled hands of the masseuse kneading away months of tension—it all gave me the space to think, to really process everything. I had been a fool to leave Brian the way I did. I was scared, selfish, so lost in my own fears that I hadn't considered his. I should have talked to him, let him in, leaned on him instead of shutting him out.

But I can't change the past. All I can do now is fix it.

And fixing it doesn't just mean repairing us. It also means mending his relationship with his mother, something I know has been weighing heavily on him.

So, before heading home, I put a plan into motion.

The first step: quality time. Since that was one of Brian's love languages, I booked us a reservation at one of the new Italian places he had mentioned wanting to try. After dinner, I got us tickets to a concert at one of the local bars—a perfect mix of music, drinks, and a little nostalgia for our old date nights. And then...

I made one last stop.

Pulling into the lot of a familiar adult shop, my stomach twisted with both anticipation and nerves. I had never actually been inside before, but I knew exactly who was working today. And if anyone could help me navigate my newly discovered desires, it was Lizzy.

Taking a deep breath, I step inside, the bell above the door chiming softly.

"Welcome in! Do you need help finding anything?" A familiar voice calls from behind the counter.

A smile tugs at my lips. Of course she greets me like any other customer. "Um, that would be great, thank you."

A moment later, Lizzy's light blonde hair comes into view, and her eyes widen before she rushes toward me, wrapping me in a tight hug.

"Oh my gosh, girl! How have you been?" There's a hint of worry in her voice, and I don't need to guess who told her what's been going on.

I smile, squeezing her back before stepping away. "I'm okay, more relaxed thanks to your sister." At her knowing smirk, I roll my eyes. "And as for the real meaning behind your question, Brian and I went to counseling, and we're working on things. I really have a lot of hope for our future."

Lizzy beams, squeezing my hands. "So you're not here to buy something for another guy, then."

I laugh, shaking my head. "Nope, but I do need your help."

She claps her hands together. "Oh, this is gonna be fun."

I take a deep breath and explain—quickly—what led me here today. I focus mostly on the therapist's suggestions, how Brian and I took the test, and what I learned about myself.

"So, what do you need from me?" she asks, eyes gleaming with excitement.

I feel my cheeks heat. "You know how I told you we took that test?" I hesitate. Why am I suddenly nervous? This is Lizzy. She literally gave me an "O" basket for my bachelorette party.

She smirks, tilting her head. "Okay… are you gonna make me guess what kind of test it was, or are you gonna spit it out already?"

She starts sifting through lingerie, holding up different pieces against me, then shaking her head in disapproval before setting them back on the rack.

I clear my throat. "Well, first we took a love language test. That was pretty straightforward. But the other one was, um…" I hesitate again, then rush out, "A kink test."

Lizzy freezes mid-motion, still holding up a black teddy with red lace over the cups. Then, suddenly, her face lights up.

"Well, spit it out!" she all but squeals, tossing the lingerie back onto the rack.

I let out a breath. "I'm, um… I'm supposedly a Domme."

Her eyes go wide for a split second before she lets out a cackle. "Okay, but why are you acting surprised? I'm more shocked that you didn't already know!"

I groan, covering my face. "Lizzy, please."

She grins. "I knew you had that bossy streak, but oh my god, this just makes sense." She pauses, then gasps. "Oh! Wait. Does that mean…?"

I nod. "Yeah. Brian's a sub."

She beams. "Girl, you hit the jackpot."

I shake my head, but I can't help but laugh. "I mean, I knew I liked being in control, but I never realized just how much until last night."

Her eyebrows shoot up. "Ooh, what happened last night?"

I sigh. "Nothing really. We're supposed to wait a few days before being intimate so we can focus on the love language stuff. But we ended up looking at a website, and I saw some things that, um... piqued my interest." I look down at my feet. "Hence why I'm here."

Lizzy crosses her arms, tilting her head. "I love you, babe, and I'm so glad you came to me for help, but I need more to go off of."

She takes the few steps that separate us and places her hands on my arms, rubbing them soothingly. "You know anything you tell me here will never get back to my sister from me. Not that you probably haven't told her anyway."

I nod because she's right—I did tell Mandy everything. In fact, it was her idea for me to come here, knowing Lizzy was working today.

"I know, and you're right. Mandy actually told me you were here, so I'd feel more comfortable coming in."

Lizzy gives me a reassuring hug. "There's nothing wrong with being curious and exploring. As long as you're both consenting, it's normal and healthy. Now give me the juicy details so I can help you!"

She takes a step back but keeps her hand on mine, giving it a reassuring squeeze.

I take a deep breath, before venturing an explanation. "I saw a strap-on and some other things, and it got me all hot and bothered thinking about what I'd like to do to him. I'm not necessarily looking for that today, but I do want something that makes me feel sexy. Powerful. Something that makes me feel like I've stepped into the Domme role."

Lizzy's smirk could rival the devil himself. "I know exactly what you need. Anything else? Maybe a training kit for him? If he's willing to try pegging, there are anal plugs to help work up to it. What about impact play? A flogger? A whip?"

My pulse spikes at the mention of a whip.

"I think... I think I'd like the whip and the kit," I admit, nodding enthusiastically.

Lizzy's grin turns downright wicked. "In that case, I definitely have some ideas for you."

She spins on her heel, leading me toward the back of the store where the real fun begins. By the time I leave, my bag is full, my excitement is high, and I know one thing for certain—

Tonight, my husband will be on his knees for me.

Chapter 19

BRIAN

After placing my order, a realization settled deep in my gut—I need to talk to my wife. If I truly want those things to become a reality, we have to have an honest conversation.

Easier said than done.

I spend the entire afternoon pacing, my mind waging a war between excitement and doubt. Several times, I pull up the site where I placed the order, hovering over the cancel button. But no matter how hard I try to rationalize my way out of it, the truth remains: I want this too badly to back out.

Restless and desperate for a distraction, I decide to leave the house. Picking up dinner seems like a good excuse—nothing extravagant, just a pasta bake from our favorite little Italian place downtown. Something comforting. On my way home, I stop at the grocery store, grabbing a fresh loaf of Italian bread to toast, along with a bottle of our favorite white merlot.

By the time I'm driving back, I've almost forgotten why I left the house in the first place.

That is, until I pull into our driveway.

Pressing the button to open the garage door, my heart skips a beat when I see Erica's car already parked inside. That familiar mix of anticipation and nerves surges through me as I park beside her, gripping the steering wheel for a few extra seconds.

This is it.

I'm about to walk inside and confess my desires to my wife.

When I finally work up the nerve, I carry the groceries inside, depositing the bags on the counter before searching for her.

I find Erica curled up on the couch, feet tucked under her thighs, lost in a book. She's wearing an oversized hoodie—*mine*, actually. One I haven't seen in ages, forgotten somewhere in the depths of our closet. The burnt orange fabric stands out against the deep emerald green of our suede couch, a striking contrast.

She looks so effortlessly at home, so utterly mine.

For a second, I just stand there, watching her. She's so absorbed in the pages that she doesn't notice me right away. A loose strand of blonde hair brushes her bare shoulder, and she absentmindedly tucks it behind her ear before slipping her bookmark into place. As she gathers her hair into a messy bun, she turns her head—and our eyes meet.

Something in the air shifts.

She sets her book down and stands, walking toward me with slow, deliberate strides. My gaze travels down her body, starting at her bare feet, up her long, shapely legs, over the curve of her hips, hidden beneath the oversized hoodie.

And then it hits me.

I can't tell if she's wearing anything underneath it.

That realization sends heat straight to my gut, my focus immediately snapping to her chest. The second my gaze lands there, her nipples harden, responding to my attention. So she definitely isn't wearing a bra.

I swallow hard, my jeans growing uncomfortably tight. By the time I drag my eyes back up to her face, I catch her biting her lip—watching me watch her.

My mouth goes dry.

When she reaches me, she presses her body against mine, sliding her hands up my chest before tugging my mouth down to hers. The moment our lips meet, a fire ignites between us—one that had clearly been smoldering beneath the surface, waiting for a spark.

I pull her closer, deepening the kiss, but she suddenly starts backing up, leading me with her, refusing to let our lips part. I feel the moment she reaches the dining table, and I know what she wants before she even signals it—to lift her on the table.

Her arms tighten around my neck, and my hands slide down her back, pausing just long enough to squeeze her ass. A soft moan vibrates against my lips. I continue lower, gripping the backs of her thighs, and the second I give them a firm squeeze, she knows.

I lift her with ease.

She moans into my mouth, sending a flash of heat down my spine as her legs wrap around my waist, and when I finally set her down on the table, we break apart, both of us breathing heavily.

"Hi," she murmurs, a teasing smile curling her lips.

I chuckle. "Hi."

She traces slow, lazy circles on the back of my neck. "I didn't mean for that to escalate like that, but... you haven't looked at me like that in a long time." Her voice is soft, but there's something raw beneath it. "I just... couldn't stop myself."

She hooks her feet behind my thighs, pulling me impossibly closer.

"What were you thinking about?" she asks, her voice a low murmur against my lips.

Instead of answering right away, I lean in, pressing a slow, lingering kiss to her shoulder, inhaling the warm, familiar scent of lavender and sandalwood.

Her go-to massage oil.

A knowing smirk tugs at my lips as I whisper, "I just realized... I can't tell if you're wearing shorts. Or panties."

I drag the backs of my fingers along the inside of her thigh, watching mesmerized at the way her skin erupts in goosebumps, the way her breath hitches in anticipation.

She catches my wrist, holding me there, eyes locked on mine as she guides my hand higher. But just as I'm about to reach the answer to my question, she smirks.

"Why don't you get on your knees for a better look?"

I don't hesitate.

Dropping to my knees, I slid my hands beneath her hoodie, pushing it up as she lifted her hips just enough to help me work the fabric higher.

Holy. Fuck.

The sight of her like this—cheeks flushed, eyes wild with hunger and the slightest hint of shyness—a goddess in need of worship.

I grip her thighs, spreading them wider as I lean in, but before I have a chance to taste her, she regretfully stops me.

"No hands," she breathes. "I want to see how close you can get me with just your mouth."

The restriction should frustrate me. But instead, it sends a sharp jolt of arousal straight to my cock, hardening it to an almost painful degree.

I obey.

My lips meet her in a slow, teasing drag, licking, sucking, worshiping. She rocks against my mouth, the rhythm growing faster, needier. I want—*need*—to touch her, but I hold back, letting her chase her own pleasure against my tongue.

When I catch her clit between my lips and flick my tongue over it, she shudders, and a hint of pride fills my chest at making my wife tremble.

"Fuck, Brian—" Her head falls back as she moans.

Her body trembles, thighs clenching around my head, but I can tell—she isn't satisfied yet.

"I need you to finger me," she gasps. *"Right now."*

I pulled back just enough to slip my middle and ring fingers inside her, and she's already grinding against them, chasing her release. I know exactly what she needs—just a little bit more.

With my lips around her clit, I double my efforts, sucking and grazing my teeth against the swollen button of nerves. Curling my fingers, I find that one spot, that *perfect* spot, and the second I press against it, she shatters.

"Oh shit—oh, Brian—*fuck*!"

Her entire body tenses, thighs squeezing my head as her orgasm rips through her. Another flick of my tongue, another slow curl of my fingers, and she falls apart completely, hips twitching, trembling against my face with a guttural moan of my name. Her juices coating my fingers, coating my wedding band, claiming me in an entirely different way.

And in that moment, as I watch her come undone in front of me, holding my head between her thighs, the thought of what I ordered today comes slamming back into my mind.

The thought of her doing to me what I just did to her. Sheer desire tightens in my gut, making my balls ache to cum for her.

For my wife.

If only I can figure out how to tell her.

Chapter 20

Erica

I don't know what happened.

The plan was to have a conversation with Brian about what I wanted to try—to ease into it. But the next thing I knew, I was pulling him between my legs, practically *demanding* that he go down on me.

And even though I've already unraveled beneath his touch, I am not ready for this moment to end.

"Bri…" I murmur, wrapping my legs around his waist to pull him closer. "There's something I want to talk to you about. Things I want to try."

My fingers slide beneath the hem of his shirt, teasing the bare skin beneath before trailing lower. I toy with the waistband of his jeans, feeling the way his breath hitches, and the shudder that racks his body at my touch.

His response emboldens me.

"Me too," he breathes, his voice rough with desire.

The way he looks at me sends a fresh wave of heat straight to my core. I slide off the table, sinking to my knees before him, my hands already unzipping his jeans.

As I free his cock, my fingers wrap around him in a slow, teasing stroke.

"We'll talk after," I promise. "But I want *this* now."

Before he can protest, I take him into my mouth.

His whole body tenses, a sharp intake of breath escaping him as I drag my lips back, grazing my teeth lightly over his length, making his cock twitch in my mouth. The groan that tears from his throat—deep, needy—is all the encouragement I need.

I take him deeper, placing my hands on his hips to control the rhythm, setting a slow but steady pace. His moans fill the air, each one spurring me on.

I needed *more*.

Reaching around, I grip his ass, pulling him forward and making him sink deeper into my throat. I gag, pull back, and do it again—slow, deep, deliberate. When I remove my hands, I can feel his hesitation, but he understands my unspoken command.

I want *him* to take over.

To chase his pleasure with no restraint.

When I'm certain he understands, I slip one hand between my legs, stroking my clit as I work my tongue over him. The dual sensations have me trembling, nearly on the edge again.

I feel him shift, and when I look up, his hands are braced against the table, his face contorted in pleasure—and intense focus.

He's holding himself back.

The realization sends a thrill through me. I want to push him, to see if he'll crack—if he'll try to take control.

Smirking, I reach around with my other hand, cupping his balls lightly, rolling them between my fingers as I rub myself faster. A moan slips from my throat, vibrating around him, and his reaction is instant. His hips jerk forward, his cock hitting the back of my throat, triggering another gag.

That does it.

His restraint wavers, his breathing turning ragged as he barrels toward his release.

I can feel it, sense it in the way his body tightens, the way he twitches against my tongue. The knowledge that I can undo him so completely only pushes me closer to my own peak.

But just before he lets go, I regain control.

I squeeze his balls, just enough to pull him back from the edge, just enough to remind him who's in charge. As I draw back, I drag my teeth along his length, relishing the way he shudders.

The bite of pain only makes my own pleasure intensify as he groans in approval.

Interesting.

I pull him out of my mouth with a pop and tsk, looking up at him. "I may be the one on my knees, but you are *not* the one in charge."

His breath hitches, and I feel his cock swell even harder in my hand.

Oh.

So he likes that.

Duly noted.

A wicked smile curls my lips as I take him back into my mouth, this time setting a faster, more relentless pace. I hollow my cheeks, suck harder, flick my tongue over his tip—each motion wringing a reaction from him. His hips twitch, his breath grows erratic.

I have him right where I wanted him.

But before I push him over the edge, I decide to test something Lizzy suggested.

Slowing down, I trail my fingers—the ones I was using to bring myself closer to the edge—along his inner thigh, then cup his balls again. I find the tender spot just behind them and press firmly with my middle finger, watching him intently.

His reaction is instant.

His eyes snap open, locking onto mine. His body freezes.

He felt that.

And he didn't hate it.

For a moment, we just stare at each other, both of us teetering on the edge of something unknown.

Then, I make the first move.

I suck him in hard, swirling my tongue as I gently massage that spot, feeling the way his hips jerk forward, his cock twitching on my tongue. A deep, guttural moan tears from his throat, one so raw and unrestrained it sends a fresh jolt of arousal through me.

God, he sounds so fucking good.

I keep going, rubbing slow, teasing circles, never breaking eye contact. His gaze flickers downward, fixated on my hand. Like if he stares hard enough, he would see exactly what I'm doing to him.

I *want* him to see.

Pulling back, I release him from my mouth and sit back on my heels. Slowly, deliberately, I raised my hand to my lips, sliding my finger past them, wetting it thoroughly.

Brian's eyes stay glued to my finger, watching as I pull it out, making sure a string of saliva clings between it and my lips.

His mouth opens and closes like he wants to protest.

But I don't want him to stop me.

I reach back between his legs, pressing my slick finger against his most forbidden place. At the same time, I take him deep into my mouth again, my free hand slipping between my legs to stroke my clit.

My hips rock as I chase my own release.

I apply more pressure, testing him, waiting for any sign of hesitation. But instead of pulling away, Brian exhales slowly.

His chest rises and falls, his entire body trembling.

I pull back just enough to murmur, "Breathe, Bri. It's okay."

His eyes fly to mine, and in that moment, something clicks.

He lets go.

A single, firm nod is all the permission I need. At the same time, he pushes back against my touch, his body wordlessly inviting me in.

This time, there is no hesitation.

We barrel into the unknown together.

I work my finger deeper, reveling in the way he shakes beneath me. His moans are uncontrolled, desperate, raw— a perfect mirror of my own.

"Fuck, don't stop," he groans, his voice wrecked. "Please—please, don't stop. I'm going to—"

His words are cut off with a strangled sound as I swallow him deep, moaning around him as my own orgasm rips through me.

The moment I tip over the edge, so does he.

His whole body shudders violently, his hands gripping the table for support, his knees nearly buckling. I swallow every last drop he just gave me, staring up at him as his head falls back, brown hair damp with sweat, chest heaving.

When he finally looks down at me, his eyes are dazed, awed, conflicted.

As I pulled my finger from him, he twitches, letting out a final, shuddering moan before quickly looking away.

I stand, reaching for him. "Bri, don't—don't be embarrassed." He turns away from me, zipping up his jeans, but I continue. "I wanted to talk about that before I did anything. I'm sorry I didn't."

His head snaps up, eyes wide. "Wait—*what*?"

With a guilty smile, I tell him everything—the strap-on, the stop at Lizzy's. As I speak, I watched the tension drain from his shoulders.

When I finish, he lets out a breathless laugh.

"I'm glad I'm not the only one who bought something without thinking today."

And with that, he tells me what *he* stumbled upon—how it stirred something deep inside him, how it made him feel, and how, almost instinctively, he ordered a toy. Then, with a nervous laugh, he confesses that his anxiety over my reaction was so overwhelming he had to leave the house just to clear his head.

"So... can I see them?" he asks, his voice hesitant, his eyes searching mine.

For a brief moment, I'm caught off guard. Then it clicks. "Oh—yeah. I took them into the bedroom. I'll grab them while you start dinner?"

Relief washes over his face, and he nods enthusiastically before turning toward the kitchen. As I head to the bedroom, my thoughts linger on what the therapist said—that perhaps we needed that test.

And I think maybe she was right. We've never really had conversations like this, honest and unguarded, about what we want, what we need.

And now, as the weight of that realization settles over me, I can't shake the feeling that this—us—might just be okay after all.

We aren't just on the same page.

We're writing the next chapter together

Chapter 21

Brian

With Erica headed to the bedroom to show me what she got today, I preheat the oven and start getting dinner ready. My mind is still reeling from what just happened.

It's not just that it wasn't incredible—it *was*—but more than that, it made me realize just how much we've been lacking in communication.

We've always been close, but we've also avoided certain conversations. And now that we've finally opened up about our desires, it feels like we've unlocked something.

Like if we can talk about *this*, we can talk about anything. I can't believe it took a sex quiz to make us see that.

Once the oven is warming, I slice the bread, butter each piece, and set them aside for later. Then I pour two glasses of wine. Just as I set them on the counter, Erica walks in, a black bag clutched in her hands.

She told me earlier that she got something else—something she wanted to keep a surprise until our date next weekend. But this? This she wants to show me now. She takes her glass off the counter and motions for me to follow her to the dining table. I grab my own glass and sit beside her.

We're both nervous. I see it in the way she fidgets, and I know she can see it in the way I'm staring at the bag, refusing to make eye contact. Because let's face it—what we did earlier? I've never come that hard in my life. And now, I can't wait for her to do it again.

She clears her throat. "So... I told Lizzy everything." Guilt flashes in her eyes.

I know she thinks I'll be upset, but Lizzy is one of the few people I don't mind knowing about this, given her job.

Taking her right hand in mine, I lift her chin with my other and give her a reassuring kiss. "It's okay," I say when I pull back. "If anyone has suggestions, it's her."

She relaxes and dips her hand into the bag, pulling out a box. The clear front reveals three different-sized anal plugs.

"It's a training kit," she explains. "You know, to get you warmed up for something... bigger."

Heat rushes to my face, but I push past the embarrassment, focusing instead on how good it felt earlier—how much we *both* enjoyed it.

I clear my throat. "Do you think we could start tomorrow?"

Her smile is instant. She nods.

"The toy I ordered should be here Friday," I continue. "If I'm ready by then, we can use it on our date night." I try to sound nonchalant, but I'm really hoping she agrees.

She does. Without hesitation.

"Yes." Her eyes sparkle as she reaches back into the bag. "I also got out the couples toy Lizzy gave me at my bachelorette party. Thought it might be fun to wear while we're out."

"The one with remotes for both of us?"

She nods.

"That's the one. I was thinking dinner, then dancing." She glances down, a piece of hair slipping loose from her bun. I reach up and tuck it behind her ear. "Maybe a little role-play while we're there."

I raise an eyebrow. "Role-play?"

She bites her lip, eyes gleaming. "We pretend not to know each other. Flirt a little. Build up the tension."

I chuckle. "I like the sound of that."

"There's more." She hesitates, hand still buried in the bag. "If you're not into it, just tell me. Lizzy said I could return it. It was an impulse buy, and it's not something I ever really thought about before..."

I cut her off gently. "Baby, it's okay. Show me. If I'm open to it, we'll try. And if I don't like it, I'll tell you." Then, a thought strikes me. "Do we need a safe word?"

She nods. "I did some research before you got home." Of course she did. I smile. "I think the best thing for us right now is the traffic light system."

I frown. "The what?"

"Green means good. Yellow means pause. Red means stop."

I nod slowly. "That makes sense."

"This way," she continues, "I can push your limits without worrying about whether I'm going too far. You'll have a way to tell me when you need a break."

I exhale, glancing at the bag. "Alright. So... what's in there?"

With a deep breath, she pulls out a black whip. The handle is long and sleek, the other end made of thin leather strands.

My cock stirs at the sight.

"You want to whip me?" I ask.

She watches as I adjust myself. "Kind of, yeah. When we were fooling around earlier, you pushed back. It made me want to force you."

My breath catches.

"I want to try it," I say, surprising even myself.

Her eyes widen. "Really?"

"Yes." I swallow. "I won't pretend I'm not nervous. This is all new to me. But I won't pretend I don't want to explore it either." I glance down at our hands, entwining my fingers with hers. "We used to be so good at communicating. And then somewhere along the way, we lost it. But after what you did to me today..." I shake my head. "You make me feel safe. You make me feel no less for wanting this. And that makes me think—no, it makes me *know*—that things will only get better. If we can figure this out together, we can figure out everything else, too."

She doesn't speak. Instead, she carefully places the whip back in the bag and climbs into my lap, wrapping her arms around me.

"I love you so much, Bri." Her voice is thick with emotion. "I'm so sorry I left. I should have talked to you first."

I stop her with a kiss.

"No, you shouldn't have," I murmur against her lips. "Because if you had, I would have convinced you to stay. And we wouldn't have gotten the help we needed. And that would have been selfish."

A single tear slides down her cheek. I brush it away before kissing her again, softer this time. Then, the oven beeps, breaking the moment.

"I need to put dinner in," I say.

She smiles, kissing me one last time before sliding off my lap. "I'm going to go wash these so they're ready."

I nod, watching her leave the room. My chest is tight, full of something I haven't felt in a long time.

Hope.

Chapter 22

Erica

For the first time in a long time, I feel like I can finally breathe.

I feel *heard*.

And I think Brian does too.

I can't remember the last time we had a conversation that didn't leave us frustrated, talking in circles just to spare each other's feelings. Don't get me wrong—we still have a lot to figure out. But after tonight, I know we will.

When I get to the bedroom, I grab the toy cleaner Lizzy gave me and head to the bathroom. As I wash everything, my mind drifts to what's ahead. How do we move forward? How is Brian so calm about not having biological children?

For as long as I can remember, I've wanted to be a mother. And after our therapy session yesterday, I finally understand that we both want that. No matter *how* it happens. Whether we conceive naturally, go through treatments, or pursue other options—Brian and I are in this together.

I only wish it hadn't taken so much pain to get to this realization.

Just as I finish putting everything away, Brian calls out, letting me know dinner will be ready in fifteen minutes. Normally, I'd curl up on the couch with a book while I wait. But tonight, I find myself drawn to the kitchen.

I hop up onto the counter by the coffee maker, watching as my husband moves around, focused and efficient.

He catches me staring. "Why are you looking at me like that?"

I smile. "I was just thinking how thankful I am to be on this crazy journey with you. I couldn't imagine doing it with anyone else."

He crosses the kitchen, placing his hands on my bare thighs as he steps between them. He kisses my nose, then my lips.

"I love you," he murmurs.

"I love you too." I wrap my arms around his neck, pulling him closer. We stay like that, holding each other, letting the silence settle around us—until the air fryer beeps, breaking the moment.

Brian sighs, reluctantly pulling away. He takes the bread out of the fryer and sets it on the table just as the oven timer goes off.

The scent of garlic, cheese, and chicken fills the kitchen, and my stomach growls.

"You got the chicken Alfredo bake." My voice is full of appreciation as I watch him dish out two servings.

He nods, his back still to me.

"I'll refill our wine," I say, sliding off the counter.

By the time we sit down, a comfortable silence has fallen over us. But my mind is still spinning. There's something we need to talk about. And for the first time, I don't feel afraid to bring it up. I know he's my partner. I know we're on the same page.

Even if we aren't completely aligned yet, I trust that we'll find a way to be.

"I think I'm ready to see a fertility specialist."

The words leave my mouth before I can second-guess them.

Brian freezes mid-bite, eyes wide. I can't help but laugh at his expression.

"Are you sure?" He sets his fork down. "We can wait a few months if you need more time."

I smile at his concern. "I know we still have a long way to go before we're where we want to be, Bri. But after our session with Dr. Parker, I realized something." I take a sip of wine, gathering my thoughts. "No matter what happens—no matter where the path to parenthood takes us—I just want to go through it with you."

He doesn't interrupt. He just listens, giving me his full attention.

I exhale. "Before I left, I was in full-on fight-or-flight mode. I was preparing for you to leave me. That's why I was so moody and emotional. I thought if we got tested and found out I couldn't have kids, you'd leave to be with someone who could."

His mouth opens to protest, but I lift a hand, shaking my head. He stops.

"I know now that's not true," I continue. "I was lost in my own head, grieving something that might not even be lost yet. And yes, I should have told you. But now I'm ready. I *need* to know."

Brian studies me carefully. "Really, baby, there's no rush. I just want to make sure you're certain."

I nod. "I am. Once we have answers, we can make a plan and move forward. I can't keep living in the unknown. If they tell us we can't conceive, then we'll look at other options and start the next step. I realize things won't happen overnight. And honestly, you're right—we need more time to work on us. But we can still take this step now. Get the ball rolling."

His expression softens, and when he speaks, his voice is steady. Sure.

"I want nothing more than to be a parent with you, Erica. And if that means fertility treatments or adoption, just know—I will love any child I have with you, no matter how it happens."

My heart clenches. I feel myself falling in love with him all over again.

"Really?" My voice wobbles.

Brian stands, walking around the table to kneel in front of me. He pulls my chair out so I'm facing him directly.

"Really," he says. "I want to experience everything life has to offer with you." He pauses, tilting his head. "But on one condition."

I arch a brow. "What condition?"

"You have to stop assuming you're the problem." His voice is firm but gentle. "It could just as easily be me. But no matter what we find out, we're in this together."

A fresh wave of love crashes over me. I cup his face, smiling down at this amazing, loving, supportive man before pulling him into a kiss.

It's soft. Tentative. Full of promises.

Full of love.

"Okay," I whisper.

He squeezes my hands. "Then Monday morning, we'll call and set an appointment. We'll start this journey together."

I lean into him, pressing my forehead against his, hoping to soak up just a little bit of his strength for whatever comes next.

Because no matter what happens—no matter what obstacles we face—I know we'll face them together.

Chapter 23

BRIAN

The fact that Erica is finally ready to see a specialist has my mind spinning.

What if it's not her? What if it's me?

She keeps talking like she's the problem, but the truth is—we don't know yet. And the fact that she just assumes it's her? It bothers me. I hate that she's carrying all this guilt when it could just as easily be mine to bear.

But until we get answers, there's nothing I can do except wait.

I'm lost in thought when Erica's voice pulls me back.

"Don't get mad, okay?" she says hesitantly. "But I called your mom earlier, and..."

I immediately stand, running a hand through my hair.

"You *what*? Erica, I told you—I don't want to talk to her after what she said."

She doesn't flinch. Instead, she rises to her feet, planting herself in front of me with her hands on her hips. Her expression is pure determination.

"Now you listen to me, Brian," she says, voice steady. "We're going to your mother's tomorrow. You already lost the relationship with your father—I will not let you lose the one you have with your mother. She agreed to talk to us, so we're going."

There's little room for argument, but I can't just forget what was said.

"Erica, the things she said about you—"

She lifts a hand, cutting me off. "She didn't have all the information. And from the outside looking in, I get why she saw things the way she did. But now that she knows more. Give her a chance to understand. You know she will."

She's right. Of course, she is.

Doesn't mean I like it.

"Fine," I grumble.

Her face lights up with a victorious smile as she steps closer, wrapping her arms around me. She tilts her head up, pressing a soft kiss to my chin.

I exhale, finally letting go of some of the tension and wrap my arms around her, capturing her lips in a kiss.

When we pull apart, I murmur, "You know Stacy will be there with the baby, right? I just want to make sure you're prepared for that."

Her arms tighten around me. "I know it'll be hard, but you need to work things out with your mom. You need someone besides me to lean on during this process."

I hate how much sense she makes.

"You're right," I sigh. "I'll do it."

She grins like she just won some sort of prize. I only hope I can actually move past all this.

With dinner finished, I stand to start cleaning up.

"Bri, you don't have to. You cooked, so I'll clean," she offers.

I shake my head. "No, I've got it. Why don't you pick a movie for us and read while I finish up?"

Her eyes light up. "Really?"

How have I never noticed how much the little things mean to her?

Leaning down, I press a kiss to her forehead. "Yes, now go on."

She squeals and hurries to the living room, and I can't help but shake my head, smiling as I get to work.

By the time I finish cleaning, Erica has picked out a movie—an action-comedy. We both enjoy it, and at some point during the film, I start rubbing her feet.

She doesn't last long after that.

Once she's asleep, I scoop her up and carry her to bed. After tucking her in, I turn on the fan and her sound machine before stripping down to my boxers. Sliding in beside her, I wrap my arms around her, letting the soft sound of waves crashing lull me to sleep.

Even with everything weighing on my mind, the comfort of having my wife in my arms is enough to pull me under.

When I wake, dread settles in my stomach.

Today is *not* going to be easy.

But I get up anyway, take a shower, and get ready. When I step into the living room, I find Erica sitting on the couch, lost in thought.

She doesn't even notice me at first.

"Hey, love. Are you okay?" I ask gently.

She jumps slightly before looking up at me with a small smile. I sit beside her, resting my hand on her bare thigh.

"Yeah," she exhales. "I'm just thinking about today. Bri, this is a big deal for us. I don't know what to expect. I can't plan for it, I have no control over how it'll go, and I hate that."

A single tear escapes, and I reach up to wipe it away before pulling her into my arms.

"I get it, love," I murmur. "So let's just take it one step at a time. Today, we go to brunch and talk to my mom. Tomorrow, we call the specialist and schedule an appointment. And after that, we figure things out as we go." I gently lift her chin, forcing her to meet my gaze. "You are not alone in this. I will be by your side through it all."

Her faint smile returns as she wraps her arms around me.

"Things won't be easy," she whispers. "Not today, not tomorrow, not in the months ahead. But Bri... you have me, too. Promise me we'll tell each other if it ever gets to be too much."

My heart twists.

All I can do is nod, squeezing her tighter.

When I find my voice, I say, "I promise, love. Now let's get today over with. Go get ready—I'll make you a coffee for the road."

She smiles at that. "Okay. I'm skipping my morning shower, though. I want to do heatless curls for the week, so I shouldn't be long."

I nod, watching her disappear down the hall.

By the time she returned half an hour later, I'd already had my coffee and prepared hers in her favorite green travel mug.

And the second I see her, I stare.

Her blonde hair is up in a messy bun, with a few curled pieces framing her face. She looks like she isn't wearing much makeup, but I can tell—longer lashes, shiny lips, a slight sparkle in her eyeshadow.

She's wearing a light pink halter dress, fitted at the chest and waist before flowing just past her knees. She pairs it with bright yellow flats, and damn...

She looks absolutely *stunning*.

As she makes her way to the coffee maker, I don't move. I just stand there, watching.

She smirks. "I'm ready."

I step forward, crowding her against the fridge, pressing myself against her. "You look so beautiful."

Her eyes flutter shut as I bury my face in her neck, inhaling her sweet lavender-vanilla scent.

When I nip at her skin, she moans, reaching between us.

"If you're a good boy today," she purrs, "I'll let you lick my pussy while I warm up your ass for this weekend."

Fuck.

My dick throbs, and I groan, pressing harder against her. "Yes, ma'am."

She hums in approval. "Mmm, already showing me what a good boy you can be."

Then she pushes on my chest, and I reluctantly step back.

"If we don't leave now, we'll be late," she reminds me. "And you know how much I hate being late."

There's a part of me that wants to push back.

But I know she's right.

I need to do this.

Still, I lean in one more time, whispering in her ear, "Trust me, love, I *want* to disobey. But we both know if I do, we won't be leaving today. And as you pointed out—I need to fix things."

She's breathless at the thought of what she'd do if I did push back. But she nods anyway.

"You're right," she concedes. "Let's go before I make you kneel and fuck me with your tongue."

I groan, taking her hand as she grabs her coffee.

"Mark my words," I warn. "I will push back soon enough."

With that promise hanging between us, we head to the garage and start the drive to my mother's.

Chapter 24

BRIAN

The drive to my mom's is quiet. We're both lost in thought about what's to come. Somehow, the trip feels shorter than ever, and I'm not sure how I feel about that. Part of me is relieved—it'll be over faster—but another part dreads facing it. One thing I *do* know: I won't tolerate any disrespect toward my wife.

As we pull into the driveway, I spot my mother waiting on the stoop. I hesitate, buying myself another moment, then step out and walk around to open Erica's door. Offering her my hand, then my arm, I take a deep breath as we start up the walkway.

"Everything will be okay," she murmurs. "I'll be with you every step of the way."

Before I can respond, my mother rushes forward. "Oh, Erica!" She pulls her into a hug, practically yanking her from my side.

Erica hugs her back. "Silvia, it's good to see you. Thank you for having us."

My mom pulls away, resting a hand on Erica's cheek. "No, dear, it's me who needs to say thank you. I've been trying to get in touch with my son—to clear the air, to apologize." Her gaze flickers to me. "Let's go inside. We can talk in the study."

I don't like how nervous she looks. Before she steps away, I grab her hand and pull her into a hug. "Hi, Mom."

Her body trembles for a second before she grips me back tightly, mumbling a soft greeting into my shirt.

"Let's go inside," I say, holding her hand as we walk in. When I glance back, Erica is smiling.

Once inside, my mom settles into her old leather chair, leaving the loveseat for Erica and me. An awkward silence stretches between us before I finally break it.

"Mom, I'm sorry I didn't answer when you called. But you disrespected my wife—behind our backs. It makes me wonder what else you've said that we haven't heard."

She sighs. "Brian, in my defense, I didn't know you two had been trying. I don't understand why you didn't just tell us."

Erica squeezes my hand.

"We had our reasons," I say, keeping my voice even. "Erica and I agreed to explain everything to you, but you need to understand—if you can't support us, I have nothing more to say. My life is with *her*. She's my priority while we work toward building our family. I won't put her through that again to appease anyone."

Beside me, Erica's breath hitches.

"Brian, be reasonable, dear."

I shake my head. "Either you want to express your apology by listening, or we'll leave before everyone else arrives. It's your call, but Erica comes first."

"Bri," Erica says softly. "She's your mom. Give her a chance." Then she turns to my mother. "Silvia, you're the only parent Brian has left. I don't want to be the reason there's bad blood between you two. But I also won't sit here and let you belittle our situation when you clearly don't understand it."

My mother exhales. "You're right. I don't understand. But for my son's sake, I'll try my best."

Erica looks at me, nodding her encouragement.

I clear my throat. "Mom, like I told you at the barbecue, Erica and I have been trying for almost a year."

She says nothing, so I continue.

"We were going to announce at a family gathering, but then John and Stacy shared their news, and we decided to wait. We didn't want to take anything away from them. We figured we'd wait until later in their pregnancy."

Erica shifts closer, and I wrap my arm around her, pressing a kiss to the top of her head.

She picks up where I leave off. "But then, month after month, we got negative tests. We didn't see the point in saying anything—nothing was happening. I started tracking my cycles, taking supplements, and trying everything I could. But nothing worked. And every single month, I was reminded of what I couldn't do."

Her voice is so small. When I glance at my mom, I see tears brimming in her eyes, her hand pressed to her mouth. But my focus is on Erica.

I gather her in my arms. "Hey, hey. We'll get through this. One way or another, we'll be parents."

She sobs quietly against my chest but keeps talking. "I was happy for Stacy. Truly. But then people at work got pregnant—people who weren't even trying. Then my sister. And all the while, people kept asking when we were going to start. They didn't know we already were. But it was like... everyone else was living our dream so effortlessly. It hurt. And eventually, the grief overshadowed my happiness."

I rub soothing circles on her back.

She lifts her head, looking at my mother. "I never left Brian to get away from him. I just needed space to find myself again—to step away from the pressure and the constant reminders of what I lacked. I knew that when I came back, we'd see a specialist. But I wasn't ready before."

My mom finally speaks, her voice unsteady. "Oh, dear. I had no idea you were struggling so much."

Erica wipes her cheeks. "I was scared. I still am. I keep wondering—what if it's me? What if I can't make Brian a father?"

I cup her face. "I've told you—I don't care how we become parents, as long as we do it together."

She nods, but I can see the doubt lingering in her eyes.

She takes a shaky breath and turns back to my mom. "I didn't mean to hurt anyone, and I wasn't trying to be selfish. I just needed time to grieve what I couldn't have before I could move forward."

Tears slip down my mom's cheeks. "Brian. Erica. I am so, so sorry. I was wrong to say what I did. I had no idea what you were going through, but I should have never assumed. I just wish you had felt comfortable enough to tell me sooner—I would have been there for you. But I understand now." She dabs at her eyes. "And I understand if you don't want to stay for brunch. Please don't feel pressured."

I turn to Erica, leaving the decision up to her.

She sniffles. "I'd like to stay, but I don't know how long I'll be able to."

I nod. "We'll leave whenever you're ready. I'm with you." I wipe another stray tear from her cheek, holding her close.

My mother stands. "Take your time. Just join us when you're ready." She pauses at the door, hesitating.

"Mom." She turns back. I offer a small smile. "Thank you for listening."

She nods before slipping out of the room, and I turn my full attention to my wife.

Chapter 25

Erica

Being in Brian's arms brings me so much comfort. I've missed this feeling. When we were in the thick of everything, I couldn't stand being held—it felt like an obligation, a reminder of everything I wasn't able to give him. But now, for the first time in a long time, I feel a sense of calm.

"Love, are you sure you want to do this?" Brian asks for the third time.

I smile softly. "I love that you want to protect me, but knowing how things looked from the outside, I think I need to talk to Stacy. I want her to understand what was going on and why I may not have seemed excited for them."

His expression is full of love and understanding. "If that's what you want, I won't stop you." He presses a kiss to the top of my head, and I melt into him.

We stay like that for a while before the doorbell rings, signaling the arrival of more guests.

Slipping out of Brian's arms, I head to the bathroom to touch up my makeup. I expect to see a mess staring back at me, but surprisingly, my eyes are only a little puffy, with just a smudge of mascara. A quick swipe of my finger takes care of it, but there's nothing I can do about the puffiness.

When I step out, I hear Silvia gushing and Brian congratulating someone. I don't have to guess who—it's Stacy and John.

As soon as I walk into the room, the conversation comes to a halt. All eyes shift toward me, but Brian is the first to move. He steps in front of me, his presence grounding me. "I'll take John and Mom into the living room while you talk to Stacy," he says softly, squeezing my hand before letting go. Silvia takes the baby—whom I still don't know if is a girl or a boy—and the realization makes my stomach drop. The baby is almost a month old, and I don't even know their name. Guilt settles deep in my chest.

Once it's just Stacy and me, we stand there awkwardly, neither of us sure how to start. I take her in—the messy bun, the tired look in her eyes, the dark circles beneath them. She's wearing black leggings and a navy wrap-front nursing top. Even in exhaustion, she's glowing. Motherhood suits her.

"You're glowing, Stace," I finally say. "Motherhood looks good on you."

I try not to let the sadness creep in, but no matter how hard I fight it, I want what she has.

She tucks a stray strand of hair behind her ear and offers me a small smile. "Thanks, girl."

There's something distant in her voice, a hesitance, and I know it's on me to bridge the gap.

"Can we sit on the patio for a bit?" I ask. "I'd really like to talk to you."

She presses her lips together and glances toward the living room. Silvia gives her a small nod, mouthing, Go. After a moment of hesitation, Stacy nods and follows me outside.

As soon as we're seated, the nervous energy inside me overflows. "I am so sorry for how I've been acting," I blurt out, my voice shaky. A fresh wave of tears threatens to spill over. I take a deep breath, steadying myself. "I am happy for you and John, I really am. And I know I've been a terrible sister-in-law these last few months, but I need you to understand why."

She nods but says nothing, waiting for me to continue.

So I tell her everything—how excited Brian and I were to be pregnant together, the endless cycle of negative tests, the hope that dwindled month after month. By the time I finish, we're both crying, and she pulls me into a tight hug.

"I just feel like such a failure, Stace," I sob into her shoulder. "We want nothing more than to be parents. And watching so many women in my life get pregnant so easily while I struggle... it's like a little piece of my heart cracks every single day."

She pulls back just enough to look me in the eye. "You are not a failure, Erica. I'm so sorry you're going through this. I can't imagine how hard it's been. But I wish you would've told me. We would have been there for you. You don't have to go through this alone."

I wipe at my tears. "I see that now. But for so long, it was too hard to admit. I was scared of how people would look at us, scared of the pity. I don't think I could've handled it. I would've snapped."

She lets out a small chuckle. "Honey, you sorta did."

I laugh through my tears, and when I look at her, I see she's been crying just as much as I have. Without thinking, I reach up and wipe a tear from her cheek, the way I would with my own sister.

She sniffs, smiling. "I thought I wouldn't be so emotional after having Hannah."

The name makes my stomach drop again. I look away, guilt slamming into me.

"What is it?" she asks.

"Stacy... I am so sorry," I whisper. "How could I not even know your daughter's name?"

Her face softens. "Erica, you don't have to apologize for that. You were going through something really heavy. Besides, we didn't even settle on a name until a week before she was born." She pauses. "Honestly, I feel bad that we didn't reach out more. Looking back, I could tell something was going on. And John suspected, but we were so caught up in everything that we didn't push."

We pull each other into another hug, and for the first time in a long time, I feel lighter.

We sit and talk for a while longer, and when I mention that Brian and I are planning to see a specialist, Stacy immediately insists on reaching out to her best friend—a fertility specialist—who apparently owes her a favor.

"She's amazing," Stacy says. "And she might be able to squeeze you in."

Hope flickers inside me for the first time in months.

Eventually, she lets out a long breath and shifts in her seat. "I have to go pump, or my boobs are going to explode," she says with a dramatic groan.

I laugh, and as we head back inside, I notice that not many more guests have arrived yet.

Stacy pauses. "I'd love for you to meet Hannah. How about I grab her, and you and Brian meet me in the study in about fifteen minutes? That way, if it's too much for you, you'll have some privacy. No pressure."

I don't trust my voice, so I just nod and pull her into a tight hug.

She lets out a painful grunt and pushes me away, grabbing her chest. "What part of 'boobs may explode' didn't you get?" she teases. Then she yells across the room, "John, grab the baby and meet me in the study!"

With a shake of her head, she grabs two black bags off the island and disappears around the corner.

Strong arms wrap around my waist, pulling me against a familiar chest.

"Hey," Brian murmurs. "How'd it go?"

"Better than I could have imagined." I lean back into him, sighing. "I feel like we're going to have a good support system for what's ahead."

He presses a kiss to my cheek before stepping toward the island, where bottles of champagne and juice are laid out. "Mimosa?"

I nod, and while he makes my drink, I tell him about everything that happened outside. By the time he hands me the glass, my nerves about meeting Hannah have started to creep back in. I drink the mimosa faster than I intended.

Before I can pour myself another, John appears. "Stacy's ready whenever you two are."

Brian takes my hand, and together, we head toward the study

CHAPTER 26

Erica

As we step into the study, the soft coos of baby Hannah fill the air. Stacy is holding her, gently patting her back.

"Sorry, she just won't burp," she says, adjusting her grip.

When she shifts Hannah into a new position, I finally see her little face. She's adorable—tiny, pink, and perfect. But watching Stacy mother this small, delicate human is almost too much.

Brian must sense it because his hand moves to the small of my back, his touch grounding me. "I'm right here," he murmurs.

I nod, glancing up at him, grateful for his steady presence.

Looking back at Stacy, I watch as she sits Hannah upright, using her hand as support while gently patting her back. Brian guides us toward the couch, his touch never leaving me. I realize he hasn't stopped touching me since John came to get us—like he knows his presence is the only thing keeping me from falling apart. And he's right. Without him, I'd be spiraling.

A tiny, almost comically loud burp escapes from Hannah, and John steps forward, immediately at his wife's side. He kisses the top of her head before taking their daughter into his arms. Then, he turns toward us.

Since Brian is sitting closer, and because I'm not sure I'm ready, he reaches out first. As he cradles the tiny pink bundle, he shifts slightly so I can see her too.

Hannah blinks up at Brian with dark blue eyes, and the way my husband looks down at her—pure awe and love—makes my heart swell and break at the same time.

The room stays silent as we take in the moment. I swallow the lump in my throat. "She's beautiful, Stace. I'm so happy for you."

And I mean it. I truly do.

But the grief of knowing that I could have been expecting any day now if things had gone differently—if we hadn't struggled—hits me like a wave. A sob escapes before I can stop it, and I don't even realize I'm crying until Brian looks up at me and reaches over, wiping a tear from my cheek.

"Love, are you alright?" he asks gently.

I shake my head. "No, I'm not. But I will be."

Admitting that out loud shifts something in me. Like I'm finally ready to accept our reality—to face this battle head-on. It won't be easy, but for the first time in months, I know I won't be alone. I feel it now. My husband, my family—they're in this with me.

"Do you want to hold her?" Stacy asks softly.

John quickly adds, "Brian and Stace both filled me in. Please know that we won't hold it against you if you're not ready. We may not fully understand what you're going through, but we love you. We just want you to be comfortable."

Guilt twists inside me for ever thinking our family would be anything but supportive. But at the same time, I was so embarrassed—ashamed of what I couldn't do. I don't fully understand my feelings. I just know how I felt.

I take a deep breath. "I think I'd like to try."

Brian looks at me for confirmation before carefully shifting Hannah into my arms. The slight movement stirs her, but only for a second. Her sleepy eyes flutter open, and I trace my finger down the bridge of her tiny nose.

Fresh tears burn behind my eyes. My heart clenches, aching with a pain I don't know how to describe. Because I already love this little girl with my whole heart. But my grief is creeping in, and I can't stop it.

I don't know if I'll ever have this moment with a child of my own.

I can't breathe.

"Bri, can you take her, please?" My voice is barely a whisper, but he hears the desperation in it.

Without hesitation, he gently lifts Hannah from my arms and hands her back to John.

"I'm so sorry," I choke out, standing abruptly. "I just... I can't."

Before anyone can respond, I rush toward the door.

"Will you tell Mom we're sorry and had to go?" Brian's voice follows behind me, speaking for us both.

I don't make it far before Brian catches up, his hand finding mine. But instead of letting me flee to the bathroom, he steers me outside. The moment we step into the cool spring air, he pulls me into his arms.

He doesn't say anything.

He just holds me.

Because he knows—he *knows*—there's nothing he can say to make this pain go away.

So we stand there, wrapped around each other in silence.

I know he's hurting too. I saw it on his face when he held Hannah.

"Let's go home, love," he finally whispers, pressing a kiss to the top of my head.

I nod.

Once we're both in the car, buckled in, Brian exhales and grips the steering wheel. His voice is raw when he finally speaks. "I didn't think that would be as hard as it was for me."

His admission makes my chest tighten. I reach for his hand, lacing my fingers through his, offering him the same comfort he's given me all day.

He squeezes once before starting the car.

The ride home is quiet.

Chapter 27

Brian

Both of us lost are in the weight of today, it was emotionally draining, to say the least. I didn't expect to be so affected by seeing my niece—by holding her, by watching my brother dote on his little girl. It felt like a knife to the chest. But as much as I'm hurting, I can't imagine what Erica is going through. Especially now that I know she's been blaming herself all this time.

"Bri, when we get home, I think I need some time to process today," she whispers, and her voice is so timid it breaks something inside me.

I glance over at her. She's staring at her lap, picking at her nails—an old nervous habit.

"Do you want me to order something for dinner?" I ask, already assuming she's going to take a bath and unwind with a book and a glass of wine.

"Yeah, that would be great," she replies half-heartedly, still looking down.

"Pizza?"

That gets her attention. She lifts her head, eyes lighting up with a small smile. She knows pizza isn't my first choice—I usually prefer to sit down and eat somewhere.

"Really? Can we get white sauce?" There's hope in her voice, and how can I say no to that?

"Of course."

She sits up a little straighter, excitement creeping into her posture.

"And garlic knots?"

Seeing her mood lift, even just a little, makes it impossible to deny her anything.

"Only if we can get the cannolis, too."

Her face lights up. "It would be criminal if we didn't!"

I chuckle. "Anything else?"

"I think that'll do it." She pauses, then adds, "I'll just take a quick shower when we get home. Maybe we could camp out in the living room and binge-watch something new?"

She turns more in her seat to look at me, excitement shining in her eyes. The idea of just spending time together, decompressing, makes my answer come easily.

"Yes, love. If that's what you want to do." I take her hand, bringing it to my lips to kiss her knuckles.

She exhales like she's been holding something in. "Bri, I saw your pain today. So instead of hiding and dealing with mine alone, I want to deal with it together."

That catches me off guard.

"I know I usually disappear into a book when things get hard," she continues. "But I think doing this—being together—will help us get through it. We'll be stronger for it."

Hearing her say that—that she wants to lean on me instead of shutting me out—means more than she probably realizes.

I nod. "I'd rather do this together than how we did before."

As I glance out the window, an idea pops into my head. "Want to stop and grab a drink for tonight?"

She nods, and I flick on the blinker, pulling into a shopping center. Once I park, I tell her to grab whatever she wants while I place the pizza order.

She's back within five minutes, a small box in her hands.

"That was fast. What'd you find, love?"

"They had spiked limeades. I thought you might like them too." She buckles herself in.

I smile, putting the car in reverse. "For you, I'll try it. The pizza should be ready in thirty to forty-five minutes," I add. "That'll give you plenty of time to shower and set up the living room."

She nods, her energy lighter now. She talks about her conversation with Stacy, and I'm not surprised at how understanding Stacy was. But I am surprised she offered to help us get into a doctor sooner.

"That would be great," I say as we turn onto our street. "But I won't get my hopes up."

Once we're home, Erica heads straight for the shower while I tidy up. When I go to put her book on the nightstand, I notice the small box of plugs she bought yesterday.

Just as I reach for one, my wife's husky voice startles me.

"See something you like?"

I spin around. I hadn't even noticed the shower had shut off.

"My curiosity got the better of me," I admit, quickly closing the drawer.

She smirks, stepping closer. "Well, don't let me stop you. We did agree to work up to your toy before next weekend."

I swallow hard as she loosens the towel around her chest, letting it drop to the floor. My eyes travel across the expanse of her smooth skin, and I swallow hard.

She's fucking irresistible.

"We did," I say, stepping toward her. My hand finds the dip of her waist as I brush a slow kiss against the corner of her mouth.

But then—somehow—I find the strength to stop myself.

"But first," I murmur, putting a little space between us, "let's eat and unwind. We need to face our emotions, not distract ourselves from them."

She blinks up at me, surprised but understanding.

"The pizza should be here soon," I continue. "And we still need to set up our spot downstairs. I would've done it, but I wasn't sure which blankets you'd want with the greasy boxes."

Her lips twitch. "Good call."

"Oh, and I had an idea," I add. "Why don't we reorganize the chest in the living room? We can put all the blankets and pillows we'd want for this kind of thing in there. That way, next time—and I do think we should do this again—I can set it up, too."

At this point, I realize I'm rambling, but when I look at her, she's smiling so big it's worth the embarrassment.

"That sounds perfect," she says. "Why don't you go empty out the chest while I grab blankets and pillows from the guest room?"

I nod.

"Oh, and Bri?"

I glance over my shoulder at her.

"You're kinda cute when you're nervous."

Rolling my eyes, I mutter, "Yeah, yeah."

She laughs, and damn if that sound doesn't make everything feel just a little bit lighter.

With that, I head downstairs to get everything ready.

Chapter 28

Erica

After Brian shut me down the other night, we spent the rest of the evening binge-watching a new show, eating pizza, and getting tipsy. He also made sure we talked about what had happened at his mom's, and for the first time, we were able to comfort each other in ways we never had before. Since then, we've been focusing on each other's love languages, making a real effort to connect.

We also finally scheduled an appointment with a fertility specialist.

Thanks to Stacy working her magic, her friend was able to squeeze us in yesterday for some initial tests. Brian provided a sample, and I had a pelvic exam and ultrasounds. That was as far as she could take things, but she promised to call as soon as she had the results and try to fit us in again. Since it was a favor, she couldn't rush anything, so we should hear back in about a week.

It's been consuming my thoughts ever since.

I *need* tonight.

I need this date night, this distraction, this chance to just be with Brian without worrying about test results or timelines.

I've been getting ready for the past hour, video chatting with Lizzy and Mandy the entire time, needing their advice—and their hype. From my outfit to my makeup to my hair, tonight has to be *perfect*.

Brian and I haven't been fully intimate since that night in the hotel over a week ago, though we have been fooling around—a lot. We finally tried out the plugs for him, which has been fun, but all it's really done is build up the anticipation.

And it has been *torture*.

Lizzy convinced me to wear the outfit she helped me pick out underneath my dress. At first, I wasn't sure, but the second I put on the black lace bodysuit and showed them, they insisted Brian would love it. And I know he will.

But it's not the outfit that has me second-guessing everything.

It's the fact that the strap-on arrived yesterday.

And it's the way he's been hinting that he wants to be whipped, too.

We agreed to work up to that last part, but still—tonight feels like a big step.

Of course, I want this. But I'm nervous. I want him to enjoy it, to feel comfortable, to trust me with this part of himself. Lizzy and Mandy were a big help in hyping me up, and as I stand here now, looking at myself in the mirror, I think I finally feel ready.

My sleek blonde hair falls in soft waves—the girls convinced me to leave it down. The fitted black cap-sleeve dress hugs my curves, and the red heels—my *"fuck me" heels*, as Lizzy called them—complete the look. I went with a soft smoky eye, nothing too dark or dramatic. Just enough to feel sexy.

I stare at my reflection for a long moment, taking in the woman looking back at me.

She's been through hell.

And she's still standing.

I see a woman who has struggled in her marriage but refuses to give up.

I see a woman who has been broken but is putting the pieces back together.

I see a woman who is healing. Who is strong.

I see *me*.

Tears prick at my eyes, but I don't let them fall.

Instead, I straighten my shoulders, grab the bag with all our toys for the night, and smile to myself.

Little does my adorably nervous husband know, I booked us the same hotel room we had on our wedding night.

It feels like the perfect choice.

With one last glance in the mirror, I turn and head off in search of my husband.

Chapter 29

Brian

This past week has been a lot. My emotions have been all over the place—from going to my mom's and facing everything there, to giving a sample at the clinic and starting this whole process, to all the fun Erica and I have been having while also feeling like something was missing.

We haven't had sex since that night in the hotel.

We've fooled around—a lot—but not having my wife completely has been messing with my head. Still, through all of it, it feels like we've grown closer. We promised not to pull away when things got hard, and this time, we actually followed through.

Instead of disappearing into a book, Erica chooses to spend time with me.

Instead of letting her handle everything, I've been stepping up and taking things off her plate.

It feels like we've found a balance, one I hadn't even realized we'd lost. But now that I see it, I have no intention of letting it slip away again.

My thoughts are interrupted by the sound of heels clicking against the hardwood floor, and when I turn around, all rational thought leaves my brain entirely.

Erica stands in the hallway in a fitted black dress, the hemline stopping just above her knee—just enough to tease. The way the fabric hugs her body has me shifting in place, trying to adjust myself. My reaction makes her blush, which only makes me want her more.

I let my eyes roam over her, from the way her blonde hair falls in soft waves to the subtle smoky makeup that makes her eyes pop, down the curves of her body to the red heels she's wearing—*the heels*.

I swallow hard. Fuck.

"You look stunning, love." My voice is rough, like I can barely breathe. Because I *can't*.

Her cheeks turn an even deeper shade of pink. "Thanks, Bri." She glances down, and I notice she's holding a bag.

I nod toward it. "What's that for?"

"It's for tonight." She reaches in, pulling out four items.

A sleek black watch. A small remote. A tiny vibrator.

And a cock ring.

My brows lift slightly as I meet her gaze, watching as she flushes even more.

"Yeah," she says quietly, confirming what I'm thinking.

I smirk. "I'm up for it." I know she's nervous about tonight—hell, so am I—but this? This could make things interesting. "I think this will help loosen things up for us," I add.

"We're always more relaxed about everything in the heat of the moment, so maybe this will get us there before we even get back," she explains, and I can't help but agree with her. If these weeks have shown us anything, we do get lost in the passion of each moment.

I take a slow step toward her. She takes one back.

Another step.

Another retreat.

Soon, her back is against the wall.

I lean in, lowering my voice as I murmur, "Good. Because I don't think I can go another night without you."

Her breath catches, but she recovers quickly, pressing her hands against my chest and pushing hard. I stumble back a few steps until the backs of my knees hit a chair, and with one final push, I drop into it.

Erica lifts the hem of her dress slightly and straddles my lap.

"Good," she whispers, her mouth inches from mine.

Her breasts press against my chest, her hips settling over my hardening cock. My hands find her waist, pulling her down so she can feel exactly what she does to me.

She rocks against me, and I groan, gripping her tighter.

She leans in, lips brushing the shell of my ear. "Because tonight? I'm going to have my way with you."

A shiver runs down my spine.

"And I can't wait," I rasp.

She pulls back, locking eyes with me, and my heart clenches at the way she looks at me—like I'm the only man in the world.

"I love you, Bri," she murmurs.

My chest tightens. "I love you too."

We crash together in a heated kiss, her fingers tangling in my hair, my hands tightening around her waist. I could take her right here, right now, but she pulls away all too soon, breathing heavily.

"Okay," she pants. "We have to go, or we'll be late."

I groan as she stands, adjusting her dress, smoothing her hands down the fabric. She repacks the toys in the bag, her movements confident and sure, while I try to get myself under control.

I run a hand down my face. *Fuck.*

"Where are we going, anyway?" I ask, trying to shift my focus.

She smiles. "We have reservations at that new Italian place. It's within walking distance of our favorite club. And I reserved one of the VIP booths, so we'll have privacy... if we want it."

I raise a brow. "That does sound fun."

"There's one more thing," she adds, tilting her head. "Tonight, we're pretending we don't know each other."

A slow grin spreads across my lips. "Oh?"

She nods. "When we leave for the club, we put the toys on. And from there? I control the rest of the evening."

The way she takes control so effortlessly is the sexiest thing about her.

"Yes, ma'am," I say without hesitation.

She smirks. "Glad you understand. Now let's go."

She grabs the bag and heads for the garage. All I can do is follow her.

The car ride to the restaurant is full of nervous energy. Neither of us says much, but the tension between us is thick.

When we arrive, we hand our keys to the valet and are seated almost immediately.

We end up sharing two different dishes because Erica couldn't decide. I asked the waiter to split them evenly between our plates, and when they arrived, her face lit up—that alone made the choice worth it.

Dinner is incredible, but as the meal goes on, I find myself growing more and more restless.

By the time dessert arrives—a rich chocolate mousse with a strawberry glaze—I'm aching for her.

We toast to us. To our journey. To everything that's ahead.

For the first time in a long time, we allow ourselves to just *be*.

No stress. No pressure. Just us.

I glance at her across the table, and the heat in her eyes nearly knocks the breath from my lungs.

"What's on your mind, love?" I ask, though I already know.

Her lips curve slightly. "I think it's time for the toys." She takes the last bite of dessert, finishes off her champagne, and runs her tongue slowly over her bottom lip.

My breath catches.

I need this woman like I need air. Without her, I would cease to exist.

"Then should we get the check and head out?" I murmur.

She bites her lip and nods.

I signal for the check, and five minutes later, we're making our way toward the back of the restaurant. When we reach the restrooms, Erica stops, reaches into her purse, and pulls out the cock ring.

She slips it into my pocket, her fingers grazing my semi-hard cock in the process.

My jaw clenches.

She leans in, her lips brushing my ear. "Now, go put this on. Make sure it's turned on."

I swallow hard.

"Meet me at the club," she continues. "And remember—we don't know each other."

I can't even form words.

I just nod, turn, and head to the bathroom to do exactly as she told me.

Chapter 30

Erica

I smile to myself as Brian disappears into the men's restroom.

He doesn't realize I kept the remote for both of us.

Suppressing a smug little laugh, I slip into the women's restroom to set up my own toy. Mine is small, more like a bullet, but with tiny nubs designed to stimulate my G-spot while it's inside me. Brian's has similar features—it can be positioned to stimulate my clit, or flipped to vibrate against his balls.

My fingers tremble slightly as I adjust everything. Anticipation. Excitement. *Need*.

Once I'm situated, I make my way out to the car.

The bag is still in the backseat, but before heading to the club, I need to check into the hotel. It's only a ten-minute walk, but if I drive, I can park, get checked in, take everything up to the room, and be back at the club in about twenty minutes.

I shoot Brian a quick text:

> Part of your surprise is ready, but I need a little more time. The VIP booth is under your name, so you can get settled and have a drink. I'll see you soon.

With everything falling into place, I set off for the hotel.

It doesn't take long—I check in, drop off the bag, and put in a request for room service to send up strawberries and champagne at eleven. Just like on our wedding night. And every anniversary since.

The thought makes my chest tighten in the best way.

To say I rushed back would be an understatement.

The front desk attendant suggests adding chocolate-covered strawberries instead, which happens to be my favorite, so I agree without hesitation. He also offers to have someone take my bag up since I'm clearly in a hurry.

I almost decline—until the toy inside me shifts slightly, sending a small pulse of pleasure straight to my core.

I hastily agree.

By the time I reach the club, my body is on edge. The walk was its own kind of torture—every step sent little sparks of pleasure through me.

I *almost* turned the toy on. Almost.

But I restrained myself.

Thankfully, with our VIP booth reserved, I don't have to wait in line. I head straight inside.

The moment I step through the doors, the familiar musk of sweat and cheap booze fills my senses.

The club is dimly lit, the glow of red lights casting a sultry haze over the space. Black leather stools line the bars, matching the booths tucked into intimate corners.

Standing at the top of the stairs, I scan the room.

First, the bar to my right.

Then the one in the back, mostly reserved for VIP guests.

No sign of Brian.

I shift my gaze—and there he is.

Seated in the back, one ankle resting casually on his knee, a drink in hand. His black slacks and dark red button-down make him look criminally good, like some devilishly handsome villain in an old noir film.

He looks relaxed, but the slight bounce of his foot tells me otherwise.

He's anything *but* relaxed.

A slow smirk spreads across my lips.

I descend the stairs, weaving my way through the crowd. The music shifts—no longer fast and playful, but slow, sensual, the kind of song that drips with tension.

The lights dim even more, changing the entire energy of the dancefloor.

My body reacts instantly, every nerve humming, every part of me drawn to him like a magnet.

The urge to straddle him, to grind against him right here and now, is overwhelming.

But then I remember.

We don't know each other tonight.

So just before stepping into his line of sight, I change course.

I go to the bar, making sure he sees me as I order a drink.

And I wait.

When my drink arrives, I take a slow sip, turning my attention back toward Brian—only to see him talking to another woman.

Long red hair, soft waves cascading over one shoulder. A short, tight green dress that clings to every curve.

They're *smiling* at each other.

And fuck, if my blood doesn't boil.

I don't think. I just reach into my purse, pull out his remote, and flick the switch.

The reaction is instantaneous.

Brian jolts, nearly choking on his drink. His jaw tightens, his grip on the glass turning white-knuckled as he struggles to keep his composure.

I grin, watching as his eyes dart around the club, searching.

Until he sees me.

His entire body tenses.

He says something to the redhead, who follows his gaze—straight to me. She studies me for a second, then gives a knowing nod.

Then, she places a hand on Brian's arm.

What the—

Before I can react, she's walking toward me. Her confidence is unshakable, her hips swaying with every step, leaving a trail of gawking men in her wake.

When she reaches me, she smiles.

I do not.

"Hello," she says smoothly. "You must be Erica. My name is Miranda." She extends her hand.

I don't take it.

She drops her hand with a sigh. "Yeah, I get that a lot."

I fold my arms, barely restraining my glare. "And what exactly do you want?"

"I just wanted to clear the air," she says.

I arch a brow. "And how do you plan on doing that?"

She exhales, shaking her head slightly. "Look, you have nothing to worry about. I saw Brian and wanted to say hi. He told me you knew about our 'date' last week." She even air-quotes the word date.

And suddenly, a memory clicks into place.

"Wait," I say, my voice a little less icy. "Who did you say you were again?"

"Miranda," she repeats patiently. "Zach's cousin. He set us up on a 'date'—except he told Brian it was a work meeting." More air quotes.

Everything falls into place.

"Oh," I breathe, my shoulders loosening. "You're the one who gave him Dr. Parker's number."

She nods. "Yep, that's me."

Relief washes over me.

I let out a soft laugh. "Thank you so much for that. She wasn't at all what we expected, but exactly what we needed."

She waves off my gratitude like it's nothing. So I do the only thing that makes sense.

I *hug* her.

"Seriously," I murmur. "Thank you."

She chuckles, patting my back before stepping away. "It was my pleasure. Now," she nods toward Brian, "you might want to go play with your man. He looks like he's seconds from exploding."

I laugh—until I turn back toward Brian.

And see exactly what she means.

His eyes lock onto mine, dark and desperate, his entire body tense. The way he shifts in his seat, the way his fingers grip the edge of the booth, the way his thighs are pressing together—

Shit.

I fumble for the remote.

He isn't allowed to finish yet.

By the time I turn back to thank Miranda, she's already disappeared, swallowed up by the sea of the dancefloor.

CHAPTER 31

Erica

It takes Brian a couple of minutes to compose himself enough to come talk to me. And when he does, the first thing out of his mouth is—

"Fuck, love. I don't think I can do another round like that." His voice is strained, his body still tense from the teasing. Then, he arches a brow. "And aren't I supposed to have something for your toy?"

I smirk. "If you were meant to have any sort of control tonight, then yes." I lean in, letting my lips almost brush his ear. "But you're not."

His breath catches.

I pull back, flashing an innocent smile. "So, absolutely not. I have both my control and yours." Then, I nudge him. "Now, pretend we don't know each other."

He blinks a few times, still trying to recover. "Right. Sorry."

Then, with impressive composure, he signals the bartender.

"I'll have another gin," he says smoothly, then gestures toward me. "And whatever this lovely lady is having."

The bartender glances at me, waiting for my response. I tilt my head, pretending to consider before giving a single nod, and she gets to work on our drinks.

Brian leans in, a slow smile playing on his lips. "So, tell me…" He trails off as if waiting for my name.

I take a sip of my drink before answering.

"Erica."

He extends his hand. "Brian."

I shake it lightly.

"Well, Brian, are you here alone?"

His lips twitch. "Well…" He drags the word out, pretending to hesitate.

I arch a brow. "Lying already?"

He laughs. "Okay, you got me. I was supposed to meet my date here."

I feign curiosity. "Oh?"

He exhales dramatically. "But it appears fate had other plans. She stood me up." Then, his eyes darken slightly, his voice dropping a little lower. "Not that I mind. Especially now that I have the chance to spend the night with the most beautiful woman here."

Damn.

I forgot how smooth he can be.

I blush, shaking my head. "Well, Brian, I guess you are in luck. Seems fate *did* have plans for us tonight. My date also bailed."

His fingers brush a stray strand of hair behind my ear. "Then I guess it was meant to be."

I let out a small, shy laugh, looking away. And in the process, I fish out the remote from my purse. With our drinks in hand, we head to the booth. The second Brian sits down, I press both remotes.

His entire body shudders. A low groan escapes his throat, his grip tightening around his glass.

I suppress a moan—but he hears it anyway. His gaze snaps to mine, pupils blown wide.

The little bullet inside me feels so good, but it's not quite enough. I shift my hips slightly, chasing just a little more friction.

Brian's groan pulls me out of my daze and I quickly turn them off.

For the next thirty minutes, we stay in character—asking each other questions like we're strangers meeting for the first time.

And honestly? It's *fun*.

Since we first met, things have changed—*we* have changed. My favorite color used to be teal. Now, it's dusty pink. We used to have different goals. Now, we're rediscovering ourselves and each other.

And through it all, I edge us both—bringing us right to the brink before cruelly taking it away.

I can see it's starting to get to Brian. His jaw ticks. His fingers twitch slightly, fisting against his thighs. He wants something.

"You want to touch me," I murmur. It's not a question.

His voice is rough when he answers. "More than anything."

I lean in slightly. "Shut the curtain."

He doesn't hesitate. In one smooth motion, he rises to his feet and pulls the curtain closed, sealing us off from the rest of the club. Then, he turns the dimmer switch, lowering the light until we're bathed in a soft, moody glow. The curtain isn't completely sheer. But with the lights lower...

A thrill rushes through me at the idea that someone could see.

I'll unpack that later.

For now, Brian is shifting from foot to foot, tension rolling off him in waves. I lean back slightly, dragging my hands down my body—lightly, teasingly. His eyes track every movement.

"Come here." I crook a finger at him. He doesn't think twice, closing the distance between us in seconds. "Kiss me," I whisper.

And just like that, he drops to his knees.

The moment his lips press against mine, I flick the remote back on.

A deep groan rumbles from his chest as he swallows my moan, his tongue sliding against mine in a slow, needy kiss. His hands cup my breasts over my dress, then trail lower. His mouth moves—kissing down my jaw, my neck.

"Bri," I gasp. "I need to come."

His teeth scrape my collarbone.

I grip his hair. "Pull my panties to the side and suck my clit."

His breath hitches.

"Yes, ma'am," he murmurs against the top of my breast.

Then, he moves lower. His fingers brush against the crotch of my bodysuit, pushing the fabric aside. His touch is light. Teasing.

I tense. "*Brian*."

He looks up at me, eyes dark and deliberate.

I narrow my gaze. "Did I tell you to rub me?"

His lips twitch.

I inhale sharply. "Or did I tell you to suck my clit?"

His eyes stay locked on mine as he slowly, deliberately lowers himself. Then—

He blows against my swollen flesh.

A sharp gasp rips from my throat.

The stark contrast—his warm skin, the cool rush of air—has me arching off the seat, my fist clamped over my mouth. He waits. Watching.

Then, finally—finally—his tongue flicks out, dragging over my slit. Around the part of the toy that hangs out. Up to my clit. He circles it, teasing, testing—

Then, he takes the toy in his hand, angling it, dragging the nubs right over my G-spot.

I gasp.

He's playing with me. Pushing. *Challenging*.

And part of me revels in it. Because this is his way of giving in. His way of saying—

Take what you want, love.

"You're testing me," I murmur, reaching for him.

But to do it, I have to shift positions. And I don't like that. My lips press into a thin line as I glance down at him, threading my fingers gently through his hair.

"I don't like it," I whisper, voice softer this time—right before I tighten my grip and pull his mouth exactly where I want it. A low groan rumbles from his throat as I hold him there, rolling my hips over his face. "This," I breathe, tipping my head back, "is what I want."

His response is immediate. He nods, understanding perfectly, and when I finally release my grip, I sink back into the seat. And then—

Brian *devours* me.

His tongue works me relentlessly, licking, sucking—his mouth wet and hot as he draws tight circles over my clit.

My thighs tremble. My breath catches. Then, his hands slide up my body—one reaching for my breast, fingers finding my nipple through the fabric of my dress. The combination of his mouth, his hands, and the toy inside me is enough to drive me insane.

It's overwhelming.

Too much and not enough at the same time.

I arch, gasping—

And then I shatter.

A violent orgasm crashes through me, my hand flying to his as I press it to my mouth, muffling my scream. My other hand fists in his hair, body shaking through the waves of pleasure. By the time I come down, I'm limp. Boneless.

Brian straightens my clothes, pressing a soft kiss to my inner thigh before pulling me into his arms. His warmth grounds me.

And now that he's thoroughly wrecked me, all I want to do is return the favor.

My lips brush his ear. "I know we were supposed to dance..." My voice is still breathless. "But right now, all I want is to get out of here so I can fuck you."

His grip tightens on me.

"Let's go home then," he rasps.

I smirk. "I have a better idea." I stand, taking his hand. "Follow me."

He doesn't hesitate.

As we step out of the club, the fresh air hits me—cool and invigorating, calming the lingering tremors in my limbs.

"We aren't going home tonight," I say.

A knowing smile curves his lips.

"To the hotel, then?" he asks, sliding an arm around my waist.

I nod.

And as we walk, silence settles between us. Comfortable. Anticipatory.

Because the night is far from over.

Chapter 32

Brian

We've never done anything like that before—never that *public*.

Hell, I could see people walking by.

But Erica? She ate it up. That's something we'll need to dive into at a later time. Right now, as we walk to the hotel, all I can think about is what she's about to do to me.

I know I pushed back tonight. I know I've been dancing around the idea of her using the whip on me. But I'm not yet ready for that. And I think, over the past week, she's picked up on it—on the cues, the subtle hesitations. She knows I want it... just not yet.

Our walk is quiet. Comfortable.

We take in the night—the hum of the city around us, the flickering neon signs, the muffled bass spilling from bars and clubs. A street musician plays the violin, and I pause to fish some cash from my pocket.

Erica steps forward to drop it in his case, lingering for a moment to listen. She's really enjoying the nightlife.

And I don't dare rush her. Not until—

Fuck.

The cock ring buzzes to life again.

I jolt, my body tensing, caught completely off guard. It doesn't last long this time—just a few seconds—but it's enough. I don't think I can take much more. I turn to her, already finding her watching me, amusement glinting in her eyes. I pull her into my arms, voice rough with need.

"I can't take it anymore," I whisper, lips grazing her ear. "I need you to fuck me. No more teasing."

She pulls back just enough to meet my gaze. Then, she kisses me. And just as I start to sink into it, the damn toy turns on again. She smirks against my lips.

"You should've thought of that before you didn't listen," she murmurs. "I might not be ready to whip you yet, but there are other ways to punish you."

A groan rips from my throat. My hips jerk forward, my dick seeking friction, my balls aching for relief.

"I— I'm—oh, god," I stammer, the need to come so overwhelming my knees nearly buckle. I cling to Erica, my grip is desperate. "I'm sorry," I manage.

And just like that, the vibrations stop.

She laces her fingers through mine, tugging me forward. "That's better," she says. "Let's get you to the hotel so I can take care of you."

And with that, we walk the rest of the way with no more distractions—no more torturous vibrations.

THE CARTERS

When we get there, I'm not sure what to expect, but it sure as hell isn't *this*.

She booked the same hotel we stayed in on our wedding night, but not the same room. We're higher this time—the twelfth floor, overlooking the city. I drift toward the window, admiring the view... until something in the reflection catches my eye.

Erica.

She's watching me.

The subtle motion of her unzipping her dress draws my attention. She knows I'm watching, and she's putting on a show just for me. If I learned anything tonight, it's that my wife loves the idea of being watched.

So that's *exactly* what I do.

She drags the zipper slowly down her back and lets it slip from her shoulders, her movements torturously slow. It pools at her feet, leaving her in nothing but a pair of heels and a black lace one-piece.

She tilts her head. "Do you like what you see?"

I turn to face her fully, my chest tight. "Fuck, love." My voice is hoarse. "The things you do to me."

A faint flush dusts her cheeks, but she stands a little taller.

"You mean the things I'm *going* to do to you," she corrects.

She steps over her dress, closing the distance between us with slow, deliberate strides. And I just drink her in.

Every inch of her.

When she reaches me, she presses me back against the window and starts unbuttoning my shirt. One. By. One. After each button, she kisses my skin.

"Tonight is about you," she murmurs. "Remember the traffic lights, okay?"

I swallow. "Okay."

She slides my shirt off, discarding it on the floor before pushing me back against the cool glass. The contrast against my heated skin is grounding. Anchoring.

She sinks to her knees, and my breath hitches.

Slacks first.

Then briefs.

Her hands skim over my thighs, her lips following, trailing soft, teasing kisses along my skin. And then—

Fuck.

Her mouth closes around me, warm and wet and perfect. The cock ring turns on again, but now she's actually using it—pressing the back of it against my balls, adding just enough pressure to make me see stars.

A deep moan rumbles from my chest. "I'm too close, love," I warn.

To my shock, she listens, pulling back with a pop, a glistening strand of spit connecting her lips to my cock.

"One of these times, we're going to flip this," she muses, tugging on the cock ring softly. "Tie you down and let me ride you."

A shiver runs down my spine, and her lips curl into a knowing smirk.

"Now," she continues, voice turning firm, "go get the bag by the door."

I don't even hesitate. "Yes, ma'am."

By the time I return, she's seated on the couch in the hotel's small living area.

I place the bag beside her. She reaches inside, pulling out a plug and some lube, and my stomach tightens at the sight. I know I can take that plug—I did just the other night. But I also know what else is in that bag. And *that's* what has my pulse racing.

"First," she says, "we're going to warm you up. Just like we've been doing all week." She meets my eyes. "And when you're ready, I'll fuck you."

I nod, my words failing me.

"Good." She gestures to the chair across from her. "Kneel," she instructs. "Arms over the back. Face the other way."

"Yes, ma'am."

A pleased hum leaves her throat. "Mmm. Already being such a good boy for me, aren't you?"

I nod, lost in the moment. The sound of the lube bottle clicking open makes my breath hitch. Then—

A cool glide between my cheeks. A teasing nudge. I exhale slowly, forcing my body to relax, and the moment I do, the plug slides in. A groan rumbles from my chest.

Erica doesn't stop. She tugs—just enough to make me gasp—then presses it deeper.

"Fuck, love," I moan. "I like that."

She pauses, stepping back. "Be a good boy," she purrs. "Show me how you like it."

Heat rushes through me.

"Yes, ma'am."

Reaching around, I pull—just enough to feel myself stretch around it—then press it back in, deeper. Then I do it again. And again. And *again*, until I hear the rustle of the bag. I pause.

"Did I say you could stop?"

I swallow hard. "No, ma'am." I resume—this time, moving harder, chasing the pleasure.

"That's it," she breathes. "Warm up that ass for me."

And when I glance over my shoulder—

She's strapping on the harness. My mouth goes dry, the sight combined with her words making my head spin. My eyes are glued to the clear dildo jutting out between her legs. She catches me staring.

"Are you getting excited?" she asks, voice smooth, knowing.

I lick my lips and nod. "Yes, ma'am." It comes out weak, but neither of us care.

She reaches into the bag, pulling out another dildo—smaller than the one strapped to her. "I thought this might help," she says, smiling.

My gaze locks onto the toy in her hands. Purple. Sleek.

She tilts her head. "Do you want it?"

I just nod.

Her brows lift. "No, use your words," she instructs. "Do you *want* it?"

I swallow hard, forcing out the words. "Yes." My voice is rough. Desperate. "Yes, I want it."

She hums in satisfaction. "Take the plug out," she says, reaching for the lube. "But stay just like that."

I do as I'm told.

The moment the plug is free, she steps closer, drizzling more lube between my cheeks. Then—

A small nudge. A slow, deliberate press. I gasp, my body clenching before melting into the stretch. "*Fuuuuuuck.*"

I can barely breathe through the pleasure.

She thrusts slow, deep, measured.

My eyes roll back, my balls tightening. "I think—I think I'm gonna come," I pant.

She pulls the toy out. "Not yet."

I blink, dazed.

"I want you up against the window," she says.

My mouth opens—closes—no words come out. I step toward the window, unsure, breath shaky.

She watches me closely. "Give me a color," she says.

It takes me a moment to process, but then I shakily whisper, "Green."

No hesitation.

A slow smile spreads across her lips. "Good." She steps closer. "Now," she murmurs, "turn around."

I obey.

Her hand presses between my shoulder blades, giving a gentle push and I lean forward, bracing my hands against the glass.

And then... I wait.

Chapter 33

Brian

My wife slides the toy inside me, her thrusts slightly harder, deeper. I can't stop the noises spilling from my lips. Then, in the reflection, I see her drop to her knees and my breath hitches. She leans forward, wraps one hand around my aching dick, and—

Fuck.

She takes one of my balls into her mouth, sucking, teasing.

A bolt of pleasure shoots through me and I jerk forward. "Oh, shit—"

She meets my eyes in the window.

"Are you ready?" she asks.

I nod frantically. "Yes. Yes, I'm ready."

I feel like I'm about to come any second and she's not even touching me properly yet. I want this so bad it hurts.

She nods. "Go get on the bed. Hands and knees."

My breath catches. This is actually happening.

I manage another nod and move into position. As I do, Erica grabs a towel from the bathroom. On her way back, she picks up the lube from the table, squirts some into her hand, and coats the strap-on with slow, deliberate strokes.

She places the towel under me, stepping up behind me and I feel a firm press to my lower back. She lines up with me, and I feel another cool drizzle of lube.

"Take a deep breath, Bri," she coaches.

I inhale.

The moment she eases inside, a sharp pang shoots through me—but it feeds the pleasure.

She stills, letting me adjust. But I don't want that. I press back against her, rocking my hips, working her deeper. She lets me set the pace, and I'm grateful.

"You're doing *so good*, Bri," she praises.

Her words wash over me like a cool wave, melting every ounce of tension from my body. After that—

I lose myself. My hips slam against hers. All bets are off. She tests a few different thrusts, searching for what makes me quiver the most. When she finds it, she fucks me with steady, precise power, pushing me to the edge in seconds. I groan, gasp, drowning in sensation.

"Look at you," she murmurs. "Taking this dick like a good boy."

Her praise wrecks me. My balls tighten. Pleasure builds, spreading from my lower back, traveling down my shaft. But I've been edged for the last hour and I need *more*.

"I— I want to come," I choke out.

She slows slightly. "What do you need?"

"More," I gasp, meeting her thrusts.

She seems to understand. Her fingers dig into my hips, holding me steady. And she *fucks* me, hard, and unrelenting, and exactly what I need.

"Take your dick in your hand," she commands. "Stroke it while I fuck your ass."

The words alone shatter something inside me. I do as I'm told. I grip my shaft and stroke, fast, desperate for something—*anything* to finally let me cum.

Her thrusts drive deeper, harder.

Three strokes.

Four.

And then—

I explode.

My dick pulses violently in my hand. I see stars, my body shakes, and I feel like I can barely breathe. I stroke once—twice more—until it's too much. Too sensitive. Too intense.

Erica eases out of me, her breath coming in soft pants.

The movement alone makes me moan again. Before I can collapse onto the bed, she's already reaching for the towel.

"Let me clean you up," she murmurs.

She kisses me before disappearing into the bathroom, returning moments later with a warm, wet rag. The harness is gone now, and as she climbs onto the bed beside me, I finally relax.

But a knock at the door interrupts the soft moment.

"Room service," a voice calls out.

Erica sighs, stepping back into her dress and zipping it up halfway.

That's when I realize—

She never even took off her heels.

I close my eyes and smile.

Chapter 34

Erica

I hadn't realized we'd be back before room service. Honestly, I hadn't thought about it at all. I was too caught up in the moment—too focused on Brian.

He was so wound up, and now, seeing him practically passed out beside me, tells me exactly how much he needed this. And how completely *satisfied* he is.

I wheel the room service cart inside, surprised to find an array of berries—some chocolate-covered, some not—alongside the champagne I'd requested. A small, thoughtful touch.

I let my dress slip off my shoulders again and crawl into bed beside Brian. The movement stirs him and his eyes flutter open, a lazy, sated smile spreading across his lips.

"How do you feel?" I ask, reaching out to trace my fingers along his bicep.

A shiver runs through him.

"Good," he murmurs. "A little sore. But in a good way."

I hesitate. "Are you sure?"

A hum of contentment vibrates in his chest. His eyes drift shut for a second—but then, as if sensing my real question, he opens them again.

"I thought I'd feel ashamed," he admits. "But knowing you were just as into it as I was… it's relieving. No, more than that—" He exhales, meeting my gaze. "I feel *accepted*. Like, no matter what I want, what I crave, I don't have to hide."

His words hit me.

My brows pull together. "You've wanted this before?"

The thought shocks me.

"Not exactly," he says, running a hand over his face. "I've always had this feeling—like I wanted to explore—but I never understood what it was until we took the test. I just knew that sometimes… I didn't want to be the dominant one. I didn't want to think, I just wanted to feel. But that scared me."

I nod, letting my fingers continue tracing soft lines over his skin.

"I feel content," he sighs, eyes slipping closed again.

I get lost in thought—the heartbreak, the needs, the torture we put ourselves through.

"I never would've guessed this was what we needed," I whisper.

Brian shifts, rolling over to pull me into his arms and I rest my head against his chest, listening to the steady thrum of his heartbeat.

"I don't understand how fixing this—fixing us—was as simple as taking a few tests," I admit.

"I don't either," he says, pressing a kiss to my hair. "But I'm damn glad we found them."

We lie like that for a while, wrapped in comfortable silence until Brian moves.

Without a word, he lifts me into his arms, carrying me to the couch. He sets me down, then arranges the treats on the table, pouring two glasses of champagne.

Once everything is set, he sits, guiding my legs over his lap. His hands move to my calves, massaging, soothing.

His tone shifts.

"Love," he says carefully. "There's something we need to talk about. Sooner rather than later."

The seriousness in his voice makes my stomach drop. I set down my glass. Swallow the bite of strawberry I'd just taken. I already know what he's about to say.

"I think we need to discuss what we'll do if the results aren't good."

I gulp. This is not something I want to talk about.

"Bri, I don't think now is the right time," I say softly.

He watches me.

"*Love.*"

That one word holds weight.

"You're a planner," he continues. "I honestly believe if we have a plan—something we both agree on—it'll be easier for you. Not knowing what comes next? That'll drive you crazy. Hell, it's driving *me* crazy." He runs a hand through his already messy hair.

I sigh. "You're right," I admit. I hate that he's right. "I don't want to talk about it because it makes the possibility real." My voice wavers. "But this is our reality. And we need to be prepared."

"For both our sanity's sake," he agrees. His hands never stop moving. Slow, firm strokes over my legs. Silent support. "What are you thinking?" he asks gently.

I blink back tears.

"I don't know, Bri."

But that's a lie. I *do* know. I just don't want to say it.

"I want to be a mother so damn bad," I whisper.

The tears spill over. Brian reaches for me, pulling me into his lap. I bury my face in his shoulder, sob.

"But?" he asks softly.

And that's how I know he sees right through me—he sees *me*.

A watery laugh escapes. "But I don't think I can handle all the needles, the tests, the treatments—" My voice breaks. "I don't want to put myself through all of that just to end up right back where we started."

A piece of my heart fractures, and I don't think it will ever heal. Not unless I get pregnant. But I know that isn't always practical.

Brian's breath hitches. "What are you saying?" he asks.

I swallow hard. "I think… I think if the results say we can't get pregnant, I'd rather put that money toward adopting a child."

As the words leave my lips, something inside me clicks into place. Even through the ache, the grief, the loss—

This feels *right*.

I search Brian's face, looking for any sign that this isn't what he wants, what he dreams.

"If that's what you want—"

My jaw drops, but before I can speak, he wipes my tears away.

"Look," he says, voice steady. "I already told you—I will love *any* child I have with you. I don't care if they're biologically ours or not. I just want to be a parent with you. And honestly?" He exhales. "I've looked at infertility treatments. They seem… like a lot. I don't want to pressure you into something you aren't comfortable with. If you'd rather adopt, then let's just do that."

I stare at him, completely shocked. I knew he'd said this before, but that was before the tests. Before all *this*.

"Are you sure?" I ask, my voice barely above a whisper.

His expression darkens. "Erica." His tone alone answers the question. Then, it grows softer. "I want to be a parent with you," he repeats. "And honestly? Watching you go through the heartache of negative test after negative test? That was brutal. I don't want to see you suffer like that again. Not if we have another option."

I hadn't even realized how much pain he'd been carrying, too.

I reach for him, pulling him into a soft kiss, pouring all my love and understanding in it. Everything we feel for each other in this moment. When we break apart, he rests his forehead against mine.

"Come on," he murmurs. "Let's take a bath."

I smile, nodding. He always takes advantage of the jacuzzi tub in the room.

I strip out of my bodysuit, and he takes my hand, leading me to the bathroom. The warm water fills the tub, scented with bath salts. And once we're in, we wash each other, then just... sit there.

Talking.

Laughing.

Dreaming about the future.

And for the first time in a long, long time I feel *hope*.

Chapter 35

Brian

It's been a little over a week since our night out. A week since we got the call from the fertility specialist. And the news wasn't good.

The only small silver lining—if you can even call it that—is that it's not just Erica.

It's *us*.

The chances of us conceiving together are slim. They offered treatments and gave us options if we wanted to go down a different route. But we already knew the answer.

We weren't doing that to ourselves.

We'd been through enough.

Instead, today, we started the adoption process.

We even talked about fostering to adopt—about opening our home to a child who needs one. Because, in the end, we just want to be parents. And if there are kids out there who need love, who need stability... why not be that for them?

After making the decision, Erica seemed lighter. Happier. Like all she really needed was for me to stand by her. And maybe—just *maybe*—if I'd done a better job of showing her that from the start, we could have avoided months of heartache.

"Hey." Her voice startles me from my thoughts.

I hadn't even heard her come in from the kitchen.

"What's with the long face?" she asks, sounding almost tentative.

I hesitate for a second. Then sigh. "Just thinking."

Her brow lifts in silent question.

I cave. Tell her exactly what was running through my head. And, of course—she's quick to shut down my guilt.

And, once again, I remember why I love my wife more than anything in the world.

Tonight is our night.

After finishing up the adoption forms, we decided we needed something low-key. A living room picnic—pizza, snacks, and a movie of my choice.

We're sprawled out on the blankets we laid across the floor, and Erica is in her short black robe. Which she doesn't normally wear for our movie nights. Unless—

I slip a finger into the tie at her waist, tugging her closer.

Her lips curve into a knowing smirk.

"What could you possibly be hiding under here?" I murmur, undoing the knot. The robe slips to the floor, and my breath hitches.

Instantly, all my blood rushes south, and my cock springs to life. She's in her favorite black nightgown. And on the silky fabric—

A stain.

My fucking stain.

My gaze darkens.

She bites her lip, looking so damn pleased with herself it only serves to make my dick harder. "I figured you'd like it."

Like it? I'm obsessed with it.

I trail my fingers over the mark—starting at her waist, moving up, grazing over the swell of her breast. Her nipples harden beneath my touch. She moves to push me back, but I catch her wrists.

"I can't see you like this and not be in control," I murmur.

She nods. But still, she presses her hands to my chest and nudges me back. I let her.

"Just sit back for a moment," she says, pushing until the backs of my knees hit the couch, and directing me to sit on it.

Then my beautiful wife kneels.

Slowly, she runs her hands up my thighs before sliding her palm over the length of me—still trapped under my gray sweats.

A sharp breath leaves me.

Then, with practiced ease, she hooks her fingers into the waistband and pulls my pants down. I lift my hips to help her, and as soon as she gets them low enough, she takes me into her mouth. My head falls back, a groan rumbling in my chest as I reach for her, fingers threading into her hair—

But the moment I do, she stops, eyes glancing up at me through thick lashes. I tighten my grip slightly, testing, and she gives a single nod.

Permission.

My jaw clenches.

I move her head in the rhythm I like, groaning at the slick warmth of her tongue, and the soft moans she lets out just to drive me crazy. But I already know I won't last long. Not with her in that nightgown. Not with her looking at me like that.

"Lay back," I order.

She pulls off me with a soft pop and settles back against the blankets. I stand, kicking my pants off completely as she bends her knees, just enough to give me a peek of what's—*not*—under that damn nightgown.

My grip tightens around myself as I stroke slowly, watching her.

"This will be quick," I admit. "Seeing you wear my cum like that... it's driving me insane."

A small, breathy moan escapes her.

"Start touching yourself."

She obeys instantly, fingers slipping between her legs, circling her clit in slow, teasing strokes. I watch. Let myself enjoy it. But then she shatters my resolve with a whispered plea.

"Bri, please," she whimpers. "I need you."

And that's all it takes.

I drop to my knees, spreading her legs further before sinking into her in one hard thrust. She gasps, and then a deep moan leaves her throat as I start to move.

"Don't stop touching yourself," I order, voice strained. "I like watching you."

Her walls flutter around me, tightening at my words, and I brace myself over her, weight on one arm while my free hand cups her breast, rolling her nipple between my fingers. She moans, tilting her head back. Then she lifts one leg, hooking it over my hip, letting me sink deeper.

"Fuck, love." My breath is ragged. "Seeing you covered in me like this... knowing I'm the only man who can mark you—"

Her moan is wrecked.

"Yes," she breathes. "You're the only one who will." Her body trembles. "Oh shit, Bri—I'm so close."

I adjust slightly, gripping her thigh and pinning her in place. Then I press my hand just below her belly button, making sure every thrust hits the spot inside her that has her seeing stars. Her breath stutters.

"Don't stop touching yourself," I growl. "Make yourself come on my dick."

I slow my pace but keep my thrusts hard. Deep. She moans my name, her body clenching. And then she breaks for me. Her walls tighten around me, pulling me in, milking my release from me.

I lose rhythm.

Can't hold back.

I move faster, chasing the pleasure as heat coils at the base of my spine and my balls tighten until I know I'm seconds away from my release.

"Fuuuuck," I grit out. "Take it. Take all my fucking cum." I groan as I spill into her, hips jerking with the force of it.

She's still trembling, her body wrecked from her orgasm, but I want—I *need*—more. I reach between us, fingers finding her clit, teasing, circling—using the slick mix of us to push her higher.

One more.

I want one more.

Her body tenses, her mouth open, but no sound comes out, and *finally* she shatters again. I groan at the way her pussy clenches down on me, squeezing every last drop from my cock.

I love seeing her like this.

Completely undone, just for me.

Her breaths are still uneven as I pull out, and she whimpers at the loss.

"Let me clean you up," I murmur.

She only nods.

By the time I return with a warm cloth and a change of clothes, she's sitting there, lost in thought.

I frown. "You okay?"

She blinks up at me, then gifts me with the softest smile. "Yeah," she says. "I was just thinking... about how much better things have been since we stopped trying so hard. It's brought the spark back."

I nod, understanding exactly what she means.

Tears gather in her eyes as she whispers, "I missed you, Bri."

I kneel in front of her, lift the warm cloth, and gently start to clean her. I'm not asking. Because right now, she needs me to take care of her.

And that's exactly what I'll do.

Now.

Always.

No matter what the future holds.

Epilogue

Erica

The past few months have been incredible. Better than I could have ever imagined. It's like we found our way back to each other—back to what *mattered*.

We made a promise to keep using the love languages and to never stop showing up for each other. And honestly? That alone might be enough to save a marriage. Because the truth is, those little things we used to do—those small gestures that proved our love had slowly started to fade over time.

And we refuse to let that happen again.

Our foundation is strong. Solid.

I glance at Brian beside me, my fingers instinctively reaching for his. He squeezes my hand, and I breathe a little easier.

Right now, we're sitting in the waiting room at Dr. Parker's office for our final follow-up.

But really? We're distracted as hell.

Because later tonight, at dinner with our family and friends, we have some big news to share.

The door to Dr. Parker's office opens, and we're finally called in.

"Hello, Mr. and Mrs. Carter," Dr. Parker greets us with a warm smile as we step inside.

We return the greeting and settle into our seats.

She opens her notebook. "So," she begins, looking between us, "how are things?"

I beam, unable to contain the happiness buzzing through me. Brian chuckles, shaking his head. He knows I'm a ticking time bomb of excitement today.

Dr. Parker's lips quirk up in amusement. "I take it my recommendations worked?" she asks knowingly.

"They did," Brian confirms. "Our communication has improved, and we've made it a priority to implement the love languages. The spark is back in our marriage."

I scoot closer to him, nodding enthusiastically. "Yes! They helped so much."

I tell her about our living room picnics—about how, when life gets overwhelming, we face it together instead of trying to handle things alone. Brian picks up from there, explaining our decision not to pursue infertility treatments.

Even though I'm at peace with it, it still stings.

Dr. Parker listens intently, her expression soft with understanding. "I'm so happy to hear that things are going well for you two." She closes her notebook, setting it aside. "Do you have any other concerns?"

Brian and I glance at each other. "Nope," we say in unison.

His grip tightens around my hand. "I think we're good."

She stands, reaching for the door.

"Well, in that case, I'd say we're all set here." She gives us a final, approving smile. "You have my card if you ever need me—please don't hesitate to reach out."

I nod. Brian shakes her hand, offering a deeply grateful, "Thank you"

The moment we're back in the car, he leans in, kissing me softly.

"I'm surprised you didn't tell her," he murmurs against my lips.

I grin, stealing another kiss.

"It doesn't feel right telling her before everyone else." I tap his nose playfully. "Now, let's get to dinner! I can't keep this a secret much longer."

He chuckles and sits back, starting the car. We fall into a comfortable silence.

The drive to the restaurant is short, but I'm practically buzzing with excitement.

And Brian? He's definitely too amused by it.

I narrow my eyes at him. Then, leaning in close, I whisper into his ear, "Be a good boy tonight, and I might fuck you."

His breath hitches. For a moment, he doesn't respond. Then, in a low, strained voice he says, "Yes, ma'am."

But I see it—the flicker of challenge in his eyes.

He's itching to push back.

And tonight?

He's going to get exactly what he wants.

BRIAN

Erica is buzzing with excitement, barely able to contain herself. But me? My mind is elsewhere. Because now, all I can think about is how to push back.

She didn't give me much direction—just a tease, a challenge. And I know exactly how to give her what she wants.

Walking into the restaurant, we're greeted by a table full of our family and friends. I give Erica five minutes before she spills the beans.

We make our rounds, exchanging hugs and hellos. The waiter takes our drink orders. And just as I expected—before anyone even opens their menu, Erica leans forward, waving her hand slightly.

"I'm sure you're all wondering why we gathered you here tonight," she begins, barely able to keep still. "But we have some amazing news!"

She sits back, and I rest my hand on her thigh—her bare skin warm beneath the light blue summer dress she's wearing.

"We first want to thank everyone who's supported us." She takes a breath; her voice filled with emotion. "Brian and I got a call the other day, and our home visit went great. Our caseworker told us we can start our state classes this month!" She beams. "We're one step closer to becoming foster parents!"

The table erupts into cheers and congratulations, everyone reaching for hugs and toasts. But I barely register it.

Because my hand is still on a slow, steady path up her thigh.

I angle my body slightly, pretending to be engaged in a conversation with John, but I hear her. I feel her.

She's trying to talk to Mandy, but every time I move my hand higher, she jerks slightly. The heat of her center is unmistakable, the thin fabric of her panties already damp. When the waiter returns to take our order, I take care of it—ordering our usual: a cheeseburger, fries, and a side of onion rings.

And just as I finish speaking, my pinky brushes the soaked fabric between her legs. She gasps—soft and sharp—but she doesn't stop me.

She knows what I'm doing, knows I'm testing her, just as surely as she's testing me. Seeing how far I'll go.

I don't have the best angle to do much, but I can shift her panties aside just enough to rub my pinky against her clit. She clamps her thighs together tight. Both a warning and a promise.

I know I'm in for it tonight.

Dinner carries on, mostly uneventful—

Except for the moment when I say goodnight to Mandy and Lizzy.

Lizzy leans in, lowering her voice. "You've got balls. Good luck."

And at that moment, I know I've won. Or maybe, I've just sealed my fate.

The drive home is a blur.

I know I drove us here, but my mind is too caught up in what's waiting for me to recall anything beyond my anticipation.

The second we step through the door, Erica's voice is firm. "Upstairs. Now."

A shiver runs through me, and I obey without hesitation. She didn't tell me whether or not to undress, and that's what makes me anxious.

I hate getting it wrong.

But by the time I hear her footsteps in the hallway, it's too late to second-guess. The door swings open. She steps inside. And I swear I forget how to breathe.

She's wearing that lace bodysuit.

The one from the first time she pegged me. We've done it more since then. We both love it when she does.

Her hands are clasped behind her back.

Her voice is smooth. Controlled. "Tell me, Brian..." She tilts her head slightly. "Did you want me to fuck you tonight?"

My pulse pounds in my ears.

"Yes, ma'am."

She hums, stepping closer. "Didn't I tell you to be a good boy?"

I nod.

"Do you think you were a good boy?"

I swallow. "No, ma'am."

The tension in the room thickens.

"Do you think you deserve to be punished?" Her hands shifted, revealing what she was holding.

The whip.

I exhale sharply, nearly trembling with anticipation.

"Yes, ma'am."

She stalks toward me, each step slow and deliberate. "Take your clothes off and kneel over the bench," she commands, voice like silk wrapped around steel.

My hands tremble as I strip, the air cool against my exposed skin. "Yes, ma'am," I remember to say, my voice barely above a whisper. I lower myself, chest pressing into the smooth wood, ass lifted, vulnerable.

She circles me like a predator, dragging the moment out. "Here's what's going to happen," she murmurs. "You're getting four lashes. One for every look I caught you giving at dinner while you were misbehaving." A pause. I can feel her gaze burning into my skin. "You will count them. And when I'm done, you'll take this"—she presses a familiar, cool object into my palm—"and fuck yourself. But you will *not* touch your cock. Do you understand?"

I swallow hard. The weight of the clear dildo in my hand is grounding, yet electrifying. My brain stutters, caught between fear, arousal, and the need to obey.

She gives me a second to answer. When I don't, she repeats, sharper this time, "Do. You. Understand?"

"Yes, ma'am," I croak.

Leather kisses my back, deceptively soft at first. My muscles coil in anticipation.

"Give me a color," she demands.

"Green."

The first lash lands before I can brace myself—sharp, biting, leaving a scorching line of fire. My breath shatters. "One," I gasp.

The next comes before I finish exhaling. "Two."

She trails the leather over the marks, teasing, prolonging the burn. The third strike steals my breath. "Three."

Pain and pleasure blur at the edges. My balls ache, my cock throbbing untouched. Every muscle tightens, straining for friction. I don't even realize she's paused until her fingers ghost over my searing skin, a cruel contrast to the heat.

The last lash comes without warning. "Four." My hips jerk, desperate for something, anything.

She hums in approval. "Such a good boy for me."

Her praise is a balm, dulling the pain and replacing it with something more potent: need.

"Now, I want to watch you fuck yourself."

A cool drizzle of lube makes me shudder. I hear the rustle of fabric, and when she moves into view, my breath catches. She's seated in the corner, legs spread, panties pushed aside, fingers already circling her clit.

My body reacts before my mind catches up. I press the toy against my entrance, pushing past the initial resistance. The stretch is sharp, but I groan through it, knowing relief follows. Inch by inch, I work it deeper, my body trembling.

"You look so fucking good like that," she breathes.

Instinct drives my hand toward my cock, but I snatch it back at the last second, panting. Not allowed.

The need is unbearable. "More," I beg. "Please. I need more."

Her fingers sink into her pussy, and my world narrows to her movements, her pleasure.

Desperation claws at my throat. "Please, ma'am. I won't do it again. Please fuck me. I need to come, I need you." My voice breaks, a raw, pleading sob.

She stands, fast and fluid. The harness is on in seconds. "Get on the bed. Lay on your back."

I scramble to obey, body taut with anticipation. She slicks the toy with more lube, stroking it once, then twice, ensuring it glides in smoothly. And then—

One thrust, deep and unforgiving.

A strangled moan rips from me as my body stretches around her. Her lube-slicked fingers wrap around my cock, pumping in perfect rhythm with her thrusts.

"Fuck, love, I'm not going to last," I warn, voice wrecked.

She doesn't stop.

"You say you're sorry, but we both know you'll push back again." Her pace doesn't falter. "Because you're a brat, and you like being punished."

I'm too far gone to deny it. "Yes," I pant. "I like it." My back throbs, a delicious echo of pain that only amplifies my pleasure.

She fucks me harder, adding a flick of her wrist with every stroke. My body is a live wire, pleasure coiling impossibly tight.

"Look at you," she murmurs. "You take this so well. You stretch so fucking nicely."

That's it. The words, the intensity, the control—it's too much. My orgasm slams into me, white-hot and devastating. I cry out, body convulsing, come streaking across my chest as she keeps fucking me through it. Every nerve is alight, my body wrung dry, yet she doesn't stop until I'm shaking from overstimulation.

She finally slows, panting. "Bri," she breathes, "you look fucking ruined." A flush dusts her cheeks, sweat beads on her brow. She looks as wrecked as I feel. "So fucking perfect, so fucking mine."

Gently, she eases out of me.

"Let's get you cleaned up."

She leads me to the shower, her touch softer now. Warm water soothes the sting on my back. Later, when we're tangled in bed, she massages a cooling cream into my skin, murmuring quiet praises.

I sigh into the touch, spent and satisfied. I'll push again, of course. But for now—

I'm hers.

After, she cleans me up—taking care of my sore back, her hands gentle as she rubs in soothing cream. She presses a soft kiss to my skin, then lays beside me, fingers tracing slow, absentminded patterns over my chest.

Her voice is soft when she speaks. "Bri, how would you feel about a vacation?"

I turn my head slightly, already knowing she's been planning something.

"Where?"

She smiles. "Greece."

I raise a brow. "And what would we do there?"

She blushes. And that's when I know she's up to something. I push up on my elbows, watching her closely.

She bites her lip, hesitating. "I thought... maybe we could renew our vows. On the beach."

I chuckle lightly. She looks hurt—like maybe I don't want that. "Love, will you grab that box my mom gave me last weekend?"

She frowns slightly. "Right now?"

I nod. "Yeah. Trust me."

Still skeptical, she retrieves the small box from atop the dresser. She sits back down, lifts the lid—

And gasps.

Tears fill her eyes.

"Bri... this is your grandmother's ring."

I nod, taking her hand. "My mom told me I should give it to you. She said after everything we've been through, we should think about renewing our vows. I was going to ask you in a few weeks, but..." I squeeze her fingers. "If we're going to Greece, why not now?"

She looks up at me, stunned. "You want to renew our vows? In Greece?"

"Yes," I say simply. "And I think we should go right after we finish the class. Before a child gets placed with us. I want to make all your dreams come true, love."

I pull back slightly, waiting for her answer.

She blinks, then launches herself into my arms. "Yes," she says, clinging to me. "Yes. Of course, my answer is yes!"

I press a kiss to her shoulder, breathing her in. "I love you, Erica."

She smiles against my skin. "I love you too, Bri."

And just like that—

We're starting the next chapter of our lives.

Together.

Acknowledgements

First things first, thank you my wonderful, supportive husband who encouraged me to take this time to start writing. I never would have thought to use the time our kiddo is in school to work on writing my own books. And thank you for supporting me getting hyper-focused on this project and letting me bounce ideas off of you. I love you, Bo!!

A huge shout-out to my author friends, who have given me tips and offered encouraging words through this process. But the biggest shoutout goes to Nina Gia!! Thank you so much for everything you have done for me to help make this book possible. From helping me run my street team, to offering to edit for me, and everything in between! You are truly an amazing person, and friend. I cherish your advice, and input. This book seriously wouldn't be what it is without you! I love you girl!!

I also have to thank my friends who offered to beta-read my book, y'all are seriously amazing! It's a scary process to send something you created out into the world, but knowing you guys got it first, and how you all hype me up just makes it easier. I love you all!

I want to say thank you to every single one of my ARC members, and my street team. You guys make launch day possible, so thank you for all the feedback!! You guys are amazing!!

And lastly, thank you! My readers, thank you for taking a chance on my book. I hope it was everything you hoped it would be, and I hope you stay tuned for the next book!!

About the Author

Katie Night is a new romance author whose love for books led her on a new journey to write them.

Her love for books started over ten years ago. But it wasn't until she was a new mom who struggled to make like-minded friends, who were also on the same walk of life as herself for that love to flourish.

Over the last six years through all the ups and downs, she could always count on her husband, her family, and her books.

She had tried to write a couple of other books before, but it wasn't until she went out to dinner with two of her close friends that an idea blossomed and took off. That idea led to her very first book being published as the start of the Second Vow series, that book was just the beginning, her love for writing bloomed with that first book.

www.ingramcontent.com/pod-product-compliance
Lightning Source LLC
LaVergne TN
LVHW012014060526
838201LV00061B/4306